WOMAN OF HIS HEART

WOMAN OF HIS HEART

BLACK BEAR BROTHERS SERIES - BOOK 2

DONNA FASANO

Woman of His Heart

Find the author:

Facebook – Facebook.com/DonnaFasanoAuthor

Twitter – Twitter.com/DonnaFaz

Pinterest – Pinterest.com/DonnaFaz

Instagram – Instagram.com/Donna_Fasano

Newsletter Sign-up – http://madmimi.com/signups/110899/
join

Contents

CHAPTER ONE

——————

"Okay, now—" Dr. Dakota Makwa pressed the round diaphragm of his stethoscope against his patient's upper back "—give me some slow, deep breaths."

Although the woman's pulse was a bit elevated, her blood pressure registered in the normal range. Her temperature was normal. He'd detected no swelling in her thyroid gland or lymph nodes. And now he heard no congestion in her lungs. She showed every sign of being perfectly healthy.

"Sounds good." He eased away from her, automatically shifting the stethoscope from his ears to his neck. "Your weight hasn't changed since you were here—" he darted a glance at her electronic file, surprise straightening his spine "—last week."

Red flags waved in his head, warning bells pealed.

He glanced up at Desiree Washington. "Tell me again what brought you in to see me."

"Well..."

Hesitation wavered in her tone. Her gaze lighted on him, then slid away. Her reluctance to meet his eyes only heightened Dakota's wariness.

She continued, "I've been feeling... tired. I've got no energy."

"Hmm. That's interesting." He kept his voice unassuming as he read the notes he'd typed in the woman's medical file just a few days ago. "Last week you complained of feeling antsy. Nervous. Edgy."

"That was then." Her ruby lips rounded into a pretty pout, glistening in the overhead light. "This is now." Her eyelids batted, once, twice. "Maybe it's hormonal."

Oh, it's hormonal, all right, a suspicious voice intoned from the back of his brain. But Dakota quieted the warning in his head. He was a doctor. He had an obligation to take every complaint seriously. No matter how dubious he might be of the patient's intentions.

"Okay." He set the small laptop aside, repositioned his stethoscope into his ears. "Let me take a listen to your heart."

He'd have had to have been made of stone not to notice that the woman wasn't wearing a bra beneath the thin blouse she wore. And she'd unfastened every single button rather than just the two or three necessary so he took extra care when slipping the diaphragm between the fabric facings. It wouldn't take much to completely expose the woman's breasts. He couldn't help but think that was probably what she was hoping for.

Now, now, he silently chided. He tamped down the annoyance threatening to flatten his mouth. No matter what the situation might look like on the surface, he had a job to do. For all he knew, Desiree Washington could very well have a legitimate ailment. Some illness or condition that deserved his undivided attention.

But the moment the metallic diaphragm made contact with her skin, she closed her eyes, sucking in an audible breath through rounded lips.

Fearing the woman was experiencing some sort

of sharp, flashing pain, Dakota made to withdraw the stethoscope. However, her hand shot out and covered his, her scarlet nails lightly grazing him. She pressed his curled knuckles against her bare skin.

"Can you feel my heart beating?"

The bold question was uttered low and husky. The predatory inflection made perspiration break out across Dakota's forehead, his thoughts splintering into jagged chaos.

"It's pounding," she whispered. "Pounding like a hammer, I tell you."

He lifted his gaze to her face. Her eyes were closed, her chin tipped up, her dark hair tumbling down her back, her breasts swaying rhythmically as her chest heaved with deep, almost frantic, breaths. The melodrama of the moment would have been funny had he been in a movie theater, munching popcorn. But this was his profession, his *life*, not a romantic comedy.

He made an attempt to free his hand... and she released it, all right. *But the next thing that happened?* Well, it was so unexpected that Dakota was too shocked to even react for an instant or two.

Thankfully, however, some ingrained instinct kicked in and he bolted for the door.

Any good warrior knows, if you can't win the battle, the thing to do is retreat and regroup. And there was no way of winning the war being raged in Exam Room One. No way.

"Lyssa!" he called once he'd burst out into the hallway.

His new nurse came bounding from the adjacent examining room. Her soft caramel eyes were unruffled, her countenance composed. Lyssa Palmer hadn't been working for him for very long, but her presence sure lent a bit of calmness the office needed these days. Well... a calmness that Dakota needed, anyway.

The instant he saw her, his spirit seemed to smile.

"Doctor?"

Her perfectly shaped eyebrows rose with her inquiry, and Dakota thought—for what must have been the thousandth time since he'd hired the young woman—that fate had shined on him when he'd found this fully qualified nurse in desperate need of a job.

Suddenly, all he wanted to do was dive into the

tranquil sea that seemed to emanate from her. But the turmoil of the moment rushed at him, once again urging him to escape.

He closed the laptop that contained Desiree's medical information and tucked it under his arm. "Help Ms. Washington, ah—" He stumbled over his thoughts. All he wanted to do was get away from the whole awkward situation. "Help her get herself together, would you, please? I'll be in my office." He started to turn away. "Oh, and don't charge her for today's visit," he told Lyssa. "The woman's perfectly healthy." Nodding, he repeated, "Perfectly healthy. Tell her I said so... okay?"

He heard the anxiety in his own voice, saw that it caused Lyssa's golden-brown gaze to light with keen curiosity, but he rushed off without further explanation.

~oOo~

Lyssa busied herself straightening the examination room, readying it for the next patient. As she pulled a fresh sanitary cover over the exam table, she realized that Dr. Dakota Makwa was on her mind. Again.

She discovered that her thoughts turned to him more than they should.

Much more than they should.

When she'd first met him two weeks ago, his sharp, angular Native American features had nearly bowled her over. Yet she remembered being taken aback by his intense green eyes... eyes that were so different from all the other Kolheeks she'd met at Misty Glen Reservation. The word handsome just didn't seem to have enough oomph in it to describe Doctor Dakota, as his patients called him. His long, raven hair had shined in the afternoon sunshine, and concern over her employment situation, or lack thereof, had creased his high forehead, making him attractive to her on a whole other level.

Okay, now. Just stop, a silent voice sternly chastened her as she stood in the middle of the exam room. Knowing her own complicated circumstance, chastening was just what she needed. There were some fearful reasons behind her escape from California. Her whereabouts could be discovered at any moment and she'd be forced to flee this job and even Vermont altogether—

The reality of her awful situation had her instinctively smoothing her hand over the slight swell of her lower abdomen. Thoughts of her baby usually calmed her. Thoughts of the child she would give birth to in five short months usually filled her with the determination to do whatever it took to protect, to shelter, to shield. And she would, too.

Whatever it took.

Lyssa sighed. The condition she was in—the condition of her body and her life—ought to have her realizing that she shouldn't have allowed herself to notice Dakota Makwa, no matter how handsome the man was, when she'd first met him at the Kolheek craft fair two weeks ago. Her heart shouldn't have tripped in her chest as it had, as it continued to do whenever she was near him.

Since ignoring her startling physical reactions to him was impossible, she'd decided to control them. Tamp them down until they were completely snuffed out.

However, the task wasn't proving to be simple. Especially since he wasn't just a pretty face; he was a man of substance. A kind man. A compassionate man. A highly intelligent man who had a streak of honor running through him a mile wide.

Hadn't he hired her—on the spot—when he'd discovered that she was in dire need of a job? And hadn't he gone out of his way to help her find a small house to rent on the Kolheek reservation?

The questions had her mind roving through her memories of their initial meeting. There had been something she'd noticed about him right away. Something pure. Candid. Something almost primal in that intense moss-green gaze of his. An animal magnetism had emanated from him, plucking and pulling at her from the first moment she'd laid eyes on him... some inscrutable allure that beckoned. That teased. That made a woman wonder what it might be like to—

Uh-oh. Lyssa rounded her lips and slowly pulled in a deep breath as she absently patted her fingers over the bun at the nape of her neck, checking for stray tendrils and tucking them neatly behind her ear. These thoughts of her boss were becoming dangerously sensual.

Again.

She forced her mind off of the sexual and back

onto the platonic and friendly aspects of their first meeting.

The good doctor had gently suggested that she might be more comfortable living in Mountview, the small Vermont town located just a few miles from the reservation. She'd only had to reject that idea once, and she'd been grateful when he'd asked no questions, only quickly promised to do all he could to help her find living quarters on the rez, as he called it. Lyssa didn't like to think of it as hiding, but she sure didn't mind the idea that no one would think to look for her on a Native American reservation called Misty Glen.

Over the two weeks that she'd been in Doctor Dakota's employ, she had noticed that the man looked to be in a slight quandary. She couldn't help but smile, even now, as she completed straightening the exam room countertops. Most men would have loved to find themselves in such a dilemma. Being sought out by available women would normally make a man happy. But not Doctor Dakota. For some reason, the situation he found himself in left him frustrated, often annoyed. Lyssa realized he wouldn't dream of giving his patients anything less than professional treatment.

However, his reaction seemed to be triggered by something more, something... deeper. And Lyssa couldn't deny that she was terribly curious about why he seemed so determined to avoid the women who showed an obvious interest in him.

She swiped the doorknob with a disinfectant towelette before tossing it into the waste container, grateful in the knowledge that if Doctor Dakota was filling her mind to this extent then there was little room for her own overwhelming problems. The ones she'd left back in California.

Automatically, her palm slid protectively over her tummy. Her pregnancy had been a catalyst for action—her child had been the reason she'd finally decided to flee from the life she'd been living on the West Coast.

When the dark storm of her own past threatened to roll into her mind, she shoved the thoughts away and let her gaze rove over the prepared room. Noting that all was in order for the next patient, she went down the hall and knocked on the door of the doctor's office.

"You okay?" she asked, poking her head around the door.

The scowl drawing his dark eyebrows together told her he was not.

She slipped into the room and closed the door softly behind her. "Dr. Dakota," she began, approaching his desk, "you look like you've got something on your mind."

He scrubbed his fingers against his temple. His sigh was heavy, then he said, "I don't know what to do. I just don't know how to handle this anymore." He lifted his gaze to hers then. "That woman... Desiree Washington—" He stopped suddenly, and then blurted, "She touched me."

Lyssa stood there a moment before responding. She clasped her hands together and gently suggested, "The exam rooms are pretty small. Maybe she didn't mean it the way you—"

"Oh, she meant it," he interrupted, agitation making his head bob. "She grabbed my hand, Lyssa. Gripped it hard. Pressed it against her chest." His eyes went wide, his brow furrowing at the same time. "She kissed my stethoscope!"

He offered up the diaphragm with its smear of lipstick as proof positive.

Lyssa lifted her eyebrows in a high arch and she

bit her lip to contain the humor that bubbled up inside her at the sight of him.

"I'll be the first to admit that no woman has the right to touch—or kiss—your instruments." A grin took control of one corner of her mouth. "Without your permission, that is."

He cast her a doleful look.

Why shouldn't Doctor Dakota's female patients have the hots for him? He was a very attractive man. She'd come to that conclusion herself, squashed the heart-pounding effects he had on her. What she couldn't figure out was his reaction to what could be a most opportune situation.

She felt compelled to point out, "I'm really sorry to tell you this, but most men would love to be wearing your lab coat, getting their stethoscopes kissed." She was about to chuckle, but curbed it when he scowled at her. "There are worse things that could happen to you than being chased by gorgeous, available women. You're acting as if this is a terrible dilemma. A problem needing a solution rather than something that should be..." She shrugged. "I don't know... enjoyed, maybe?"

His deep frown told her he thought her suggestion was outrageous. Repugnant, even.

Lyssa didn't bother to quell the laughter bubbling up from the back of her throat. He needed to be laughed at. He was taking himself and what he saw as a predicament much too seriously.

"I'm sorry, if you don't agree with me," she told him. "But as I see it, you've got two options. You can go with the flow... which means taking some of these women out on a date or two to see if something more develops. Or—" she lifted her shoulders again "—you can take yourself off the market."

Yes, she'd made light of what he'd obviously perceived to be a problem, but she'd only told him exactly what she felt he needed to hear. As she walked down the hallway toward the waiting room, Lyssa glanced out the nearby window, enjoying the autumn colors that tinged the leaves and she didn't give her words a second thought. She'd simply helped her boss put things into perspective. However, she hadn't witnessed the acute interest that lit the doctor's eyes. She hadn't observed the thoughtful expression that had overtaken his every feature. She hadn't seen the way he'd unwittingly begun to tap the pad of his index finger against his chin as he pondered.

If she'd been the least bit aware of his powerful reactions to the choices she'd offered him—the final one, in particular—she'd have realized that his life was about to change.

As was hers.

Forever.

~oOo~

Dakota Makwa's nerves were a jumbled mess as he reached up and knocked on the door of the small, wood-frame bungalow that Lyssa rented. He hoped he wouldn't be disturbing her dinner, but he just couldn't wait any longer to talk to her.

The suggestion she'd made in his office today had turned into an amazing epiphany for him, and he felt that if he didn't talk to her about his decisions now, he would bust at the seams with all the thoughts that continued to churn in his head.

"Doctor Dakota?"

The pleasant surprise in both her soft brown gaze and in her tone touched the very heart of him. He didn't know a whole lot about Lyssa Palmer, but he'd discovered she was skilled at her profession.

She cared about the patients. She was a good person.

When she'd taken the job as a nurse in his medical office, she'd made him aware of the basic facts of her life: she was pregnant, newly divorced, and on the run from the man she'd called husband for a year and a half. She'd offered nothing more. He'd have liked for her to be more open about her history, but he had easily understood her reluctance to reveal too much, so he'd decided early on to practice patience in dealing with his new employee.

He'd been in desperate need of a nurse. And she'd been in desperate need of a job. That had to be enough for the moment. Eventually, he'd hoped, she'd tell him about her past. Once she learned he was worthy of her trust. Until then, he would be satisfied with the information she was willing to offer.

As he stood there, her beautiful face shadowed with what he took to be concern.

"Is everything all right?" She glanced around as if she feared trouble was close at hand.

Her vulnerability affected him. Deeply. Surprisingly. And he felt compelled to assure her. "Everything's fine, Lyssa. I hope I'm not bothering you. But I just have to talk."

He felt more than a little awkward about barging into her home, but he'd come to discuss a matter of the most personal nature. A matter he didn't want overheard by his receptionist, his patients, or anyone else for that matter.

"Come in," she told him, holding the door open for him.

The tiny, sparsely furnished living room housed a love seat and a matching chair, one side table and a lamp. The kitchenette was clean, the counters clear. No knickknacks cluttered the surfaces, and Dakota didn't know if that was because she preferred things that way, or if she couldn't afford the luxuries of ornamental accessories, or if she wished to keep her life uncomplicated just in case she needed to move on in a hurry.

He hoped her home was decorated the way it was because she liked her life neat and tidy, but he highly suspected that one of the other reasons was probably the cause. Dakota couldn't help but note the sad tone that seemed to hum in the room. A lonely, almost depressing air. And that stunned him because the Lyssa he'd come to know over the past couple of weeks was very positive and upbeat.

"Can I offer you something?" she asked. "A glass of iced tea?"

"Nothing, thanks," he said. Then he was again stricken with an overwhelming nervousness as he wondered how she'd react to what he was about to suggest. He stuffed his hands deep into his trouser pockets.

When he didn't speak and was unable to meet her eyes, she asked, "Is there something wrong with my work? You're not here to fire me, are you? I'm terribly sorry if I've done something—"

"No, no." He shook his head, the frantic quality in her voice making his gaze shoot to hers. "It's not that at all. I'm happy with your work. You're a very capable nurse. A terrific benefit to my staff. I mean that. I do."

She needed this job, he knew that. And he needed her in it, so he was more than happy to appease her anxiety. What had him on edge was how he should go about proposing his radical idea to her.

Proposing. What an interesting choice of verbs his subconscious had produced.

"I'm here," he began, "because of something you said to me today."

Apparently, the compliments he'd offered on her talents as a nurse hadn't completely alleviated her apprehension.

"I sure didn't mean to say anything to upset you." There it was again. That self-blaming regret in her words, in her posture. Lyssa apologized much too often. However, his curiosity regarding why that might be was overridden by the task at hand.

"You didn't upset me," he rushed to add, wanting to set her mind at rest. He tried again, "But what you said today at the office did, um, have a great impact on me." Again, nerves had him going silent.

Worry tensed her expression. "Doctor Dakota, it's obvious that I've troubled you in some way, and I do apologize—"

He cut her off with a firm shake of his head. Then he heaved a sigh. "It's not you. It's me. I'm not going at this very well." He offered a quirky smile in an effort to let her know all was well.

Finally, she eased down onto the chair and said,

"Maybe you should sit down and tell me what it was I said that has you so rattled."

His smile widened and eased. Yes. He should sit, relax, and reveal his idea.

Once he was settled on the love seat, he inched to the edge and rested his elbows on his knees. "You told me today that I should take myself off the market."

Surprise rounded her eyes attractively. He didn't want to think of Lyssa as appealing. Heck, with his track record, he didn't want to think of any woman as alluring. But he'd be lying to himself if he said Lyssa Palmer wasn't anything other than what she was... striking.

Then her wide, full mouth pulled back in a smile. "Yes, but I was joking when I said that. I was serious about you taking some of those ladies out on a few dates. It's not going to kill you to get to know them. You never know, you just may end up—"

"I can't do that," he said, unable to stop the curtness in his voice. "I could use propriety as an excuse... but my reasons are more than merely professional ethics."

Her jaw snapped shut and her curiosity became evident.

"I'd like to offer you an explanation," he told her, "but my sob story would be long and tedious. Just know that dating any of those women is out of the question for me."

Rather than quenching her interest, his response only seemed to sharpen her curiosity. But that couldn't be helped. His past wasn't what he came here to talk about. His future—their future—was what was important at the moment.

"You told me today," he continued, "that taking myself off the market, making myself unavailable, was one of my choices in dealing with my, um, problem. And I've come to the unequivocal conclusion that I agree."

"But I just told you that I was teasing you when I made that suggestion," she reminded him.

"Ignore that point," he said, "It's the only viable option that I can see." He ran an agitated hand over his jaw. "Lyssa, those women are going to drive me nuts. I've got to find a way to avoid... well, to avoid all this nonsense. It's affecting the whole practice. And I can't stand it."

She was quiet for a moment. When she spoke, her words were soft but firm.

"I don't understand why you just don't tell Desiree Washington that you don't enjoy her flirting."

"Don't you think I've tried that?" Frustration frayed his wits. "Not three weeks ago, I looked that woman in the face and told her, point-blank, that I'm not interested. In her or in anyone else. But she didn't believe me. Or she refused to listen. Or she thought she could change my mind."

Lyssa grimaced. "She's a woman. Women always think they can change men." Then her mouth twisted before she softly whispered, "But we're always dead wrong."

There was much more to that aside, but he was too preoccupied with his own problem to give her insinuation the due attention it deserved.

"Desiree's not the only one," he felt the need to inform her. "There are others."

"Yes, I work in that office. I've noticed." She tipped up her chin. "Maybe you should just be a little more forceful in making your feelings known. If these women can't understand subtle hints, if they can't take your resolute but gentle rejection, then maybe you need to introduce them to Dr. Nasty. Don't be so protective of their feelings. Once they experience the sting of some harsh disdain, then maybe they won't be so quick to make such blatant passes at you."

Oh, how he wished he could give Desiree Washington and a couple of his other female patients a piece of his mind. Release Dr. Nasty, as Lyssa was suggesting. Telling those women exactly how he felt about them and their behavior would really feel good.

But he shook his head. "I can't do that, Lyssa. I just can't. You see, my grandfather taught me that I should promote integrity in all things. I don't know if you'll understand this, but that teaching is more than just a philosophy of life. It's a universal truth. The Kolheek way. I am to respect others. I must treat them how I want to be treated."

"But, Doctor Dakota, they're not respecting you." Her eyebrows shot heavenward as she made her point.

His tone quieted as he explained, "They have to resolve that with The Great One on the Day of Reckoning. I only have to atone for my own actions."

Over the course of his life, he'd encountered many people who had scoffed at his Kolheek traditions. Many of his friends—people who hadn't been raised on the rez, hadn't grown up listening to the stories and lessons of The People—believed that his beliefs were elementary. Even antiquated. But Dakota was proud of who he was, proud of the heritage and teachings on which he strived to base his life.

He'd fully expected Lyssa's brown gaze to light with humor, but it didn't. In fact, what he saw on her face was a sense of respect.

"Okay," she said softly, "so if you can't put these women in their place with some good old-fashioned humiliation—which is exactly what they deserve, if you ask me—then I guess you do have to make yourself unavailable to them." She paused for only a second before she continued, "I guess that means you have to find yourself a long-term girlfriend."

Now that her thinking was more along the lines of his, he shook his head, wanting to nudge her completely onto the path he'd paved for himself earlier today. "I'm interested in something a little

more concrete than that. Something a little more...
definitive."

Total surprise lit her delicate features. "M-
marriage?"

"Exactly!" he said. And before he lost his nerve,
he added, "I was hoping you'd agree to become my
wife."

CHAPTER TWO

————

Lyssa laughed. "Yeah, right. Sure thing, doc." She patted her rounded belly. "Not too sure I can get away with wearing white, though."

But he didn't laugh with her. In fact, he didn't even smile.

"Wait." Every ounce of humor evaporated. "You're serious?"

"Completely."

She blinked. "Have you lost your mind?"

She hadn't meant to snap at her boss, but the man had clearly lost his mind. Once she'd had a chance to take a calming breath, she began, "Dr. Dakota..."

But the rest of her thought was dissolved away

by the sudden and wholly enthusiastic twinkle lighting his mossy gaze. And what a sexy gaze it was! Her heart pattered like the wings of a hummingbird and her thoughts churned up all sorts of precarious notions. Such as what would those soft, dusky lips of his feel like against her own as they shared a kiss at the altar like real brides and grooms do?

Stop! Luckily, the silent voice in her head had sense enough to cut off the thought. She already had more problems than she could handle. She refused to add to them by toying with an attraction to the one man who had been good enough to offer her a job when she'd been in such dire need of employment.

Lyssa took a deep breath and forced herself to calm down. She lifted her gaze to his. "I'm not sure you've thought this through, Dr. Dakota."

The small smile that hovered at the corners of his mouth widened into a confident grin, and she was relieved that she was sitting down. That smile was too inviting for words. His silly suggestion overwhelmed her. Had she been standing, her wobbly knees wouldn't have supported her weight.

"Don't you think you should drop the 'doctor'?"

he asked. "Call me Dakota. I think our relationship is evolving to a new level, don't you?"

She shook her head. "No. No, I absolutely do not."

The confidence on his handsome face waned a fraction.

"Dr. Dakota, I can see your problem. Honestly, I can. I've seen the patients coming into the office in leopard-spotted undies and glitter powder in the strangest of places. And I understand how you might believe that finding a wife would be the solution to that problem..." She felt the over-powering need to swallow, but discovered that her mouth had gone bone-dry. "But I don't understand why you've asked me?" She pressed her open palm to her chest. "I'm divorced. I'm pregnant. I'm... well—" without thought, her voice lowered to a conspiratorial tone "—I'm *hiding* from my ex-husband. My life is total disaster-on-a-stick at the moment."

"I know all that," Dakota said easily. "And that's why I chose you."

She wasn't a stupid woman, but for the life of her she couldn't seem to get her brain to wrap itself around his logic. Frustration clipped her tone as she asked, "What do you mean? All those facts should have you running for the hills, not asking me to be your wife."

His full, sensuous lips pressed together, and once again Lyssa couldn't help but wonder what his kiss might taste like if—

Aaarrgg! Stop, stop, stop! Again that frustrated voice kicked in, and Lyssa felt terrifically indebted by its silent chastisement... but she'd feel less off balance if she could force herself to surrender to her own common sense.

"I'll be happy to explain," he said.

He scooted forward on the seat and reached out to take her hand. His skin was warm against her own and only served to further muddle her frantic thoughts.

"You haven't said much about your past." Then he rushed to add, "And I'm not asking you to disclose anything you aren't comfortable with. But since I do know that you're... well, that you're on the lam, so to speak, I think this marriage I'm proposing would be good for both of us. It'll keep me safe from those women who are, well, intent on hog-tying me. And it'll make you harder to find."

Confusion had her thoughts clashing like

thunder clouds. It was both the astounding topic of conversation, Lyssa knew, and the fact that the pad of Dakota's thumb roved in small semicircles over her skin. She couldn't think coherently.

He lifted one shoulder. "You'll take my name. You won't be Lyssa Palmer any longer. You'll be Lyssa Makwa. You'll be safe. Well," he amended, "safer, anyway. I want you to know, Lyssa, I'll do everything in my power to protect you. To protect your child."

The turmoil she was experiencing waned as poignant emotion clogged her throat like a fat rope that had been knotted several times over.

Oh, Lord, how she'd have loved to believe him! It had been a long time since she'd felt protected and cared for. There was a warm and fuzzy coddling in his declaration that sounded downright delectable. But after all she'd been through, Lyssa didn't dare trust her own safety or the safety of her baby to anyone. Dakota's promise was enough to melt her heart to the point that it was dripping like hot wax down her ribs. But he didn't know the whole story. He hadn't a clue what he was asking to get involved in. He had no idea of the magnitude of what, of who, she was running from. If he did, he surely wouldn't be making promises. He surely wouldn't want to have anything to do with her. The right thing for her to do was to save him from his own ignorance.

She tried to tug her hand free. Thinking clearly was impossible with the heat of him against her flesh. "Dr. Dakota, Tori just introduced us two short weeks ago."

Lyssa thought it would have been great to talk to the calm, collected Tori about this disastrous idea of Dakota's. Victoria Landing, better known as Tori, owned the bed and breakfast where Lyssa had stayed when she'd first arrived in Vermont. The woman had become a true and trusted friend to Lyssa.

"I realize that. And I don't want you to think I'm suggesting anything improper here."

For some reason, Lyssa instinctively knew he wasn't.

"I'm talking a strictly platonic relationship," he assured her. "A union that will benefit both of us."

For one quick moment, Lyssa allowed herself to imagine what it might be like to be married to a man like Dakota Makwa. He was mature in his thinking. He was smart. He was kind and

31

concerned about the feelings of others almost to the point of seeming to be too altruistic. That wasn't a bad thing. That was a wonderful thing. Because it made Dakota the exact opposite of her ex.

Being Dakota's wife would bring some wondrous advantages, she was certain. Her eyes wandered to where his fingers moseyed over her skin, lifted to his sexy mouth. Naughty images danced in her brain and made her body flush with heat.

Sucking in a huge gasp, she stood up, jerking her hand from his.

"This is *crazy*," she told him. "You can't do this. It's too much. Too extreme. Marriage is not the answer to your problem, do you hear me?"

It would not be fair to him to involve him in her problem. Of that, she was certain. With that thought in mind, she reached out and took hold of his sleeve, tugging him up from where he sat.

"Besides that... you don't know what you're proposing," she murmured, her mind spinning but resolved, as she herded him toward the door. "You have no idea what you'd be getting mixed up in. I won't let you do this. I just won't."

Ignoring the startled look in his deep-green eyes, she nudged at him until she succeeded in getting him outside on her front porch. And then she closed the door, breathing a sigh of relief to know that he and his outlandish suggestion were safely on the other side.

Her chest heaved as she rested her forehead against the worn paint on the door jamb and closed her eyes. Finally, she risked a quick peek out the front window, her heart paining when she saw Dakota walking away, his dark hair a shiny curtain down his back, his shoulders rounded in defeat.

But only a moment later she tipped up her chin with confidence.

"I've done the right thing," she whispered aloud. It didn't matter that there was no one to hear. "He might not think so right now. But I *know* I've done the right thing."

The next two days were awkward ones at the office. Doctor Dakota's apology had been stiff and Lyssa's acceptance of it had felt just as unwieldy. She'd hoped that would be the end of it, but his proposal of marriage had stirred something between them. An acute awareness that was quite startling.

Oh, she'd noticed Doctor Dakota before his outrageous proposal. There could be no denying that. But she wasn't alone. His tall, athletic frame had caught the eye of every unattached woman at Misty Glen, and a handful of those from the nearby town, as well. His high cheekbones, those intelligent loden-green eyes, all that long, dark hair...

The man should be modeling designer suits on the cover of GQ and Esquire, not stuck in the sparsely populated mountains of Vermont practicing medicine on a Native American reservation.

So, yes, she'd admit it. She'd felt an attraction. However, she'd done a marvelous job of controlling herself. Also, she hadn't had the feeling, before now, that he'd done much noticing of her. Now that Doctor Dakota had asked her to marry him, though, all that had changed.

Whenever Lyssa found herself working in an exam room with him, the walls seemed to close in until there wasn't enough space to maneuver. Their shoulders and arms were constantly brushing, or she'd snag the hem of his lab coat as she walked by him in the hallway. Those occurrences hadn't seemed a problem before.

And that gaze of his... it always seemed to be watching her now. Following her when she least expected. The intensity in his eyes was unnerving. The expression in them never the same. He'd look intrigued one moment—although she couldn't fathom what on earth he'd have to feel intrigued about—the next he'd look frustrated, and the next he'd actually seem annoyed. Then there were those times when she hadn't been able to tell what he was thinking, his expression would be so unfathomable.

She wished he hadn't shown up on her doorstep. She wished he hadn't made her a part of his silly, impossible plan.

No, what she really wished was that she'd never made that remark about him solving his problems by making himself unavailable to the women who so blatantly wanted him. This was *her* fault.

Why was it, she wondered, that she always seemed to be her own worse enemy?

Sighing, she continued the task of refilling the supply cabinet, her thoughts in bedlam. She'd told him the truth when she'd said he had no idea what he'd be getting involved with her. He'd put himself and his career in enough peril by just helping her get away from Rodney and his family in California—

"Lyssa!"

Dr. Dakota's sharp tone nearly made her jump out of her skin and boxes of bandages flew, helter-skelter, tumbling onto the floor. She didn't just rush, she ran down the hallway. He was coming out of the exam room at the very end of the hallway just as she arrived on the scene, his handsome face drawn tight.

"Take care of that," he barked.

Fire smoldered in his eyes as he stormed away toward his office. And was that a touch of accusation simmering in his gaze? She slipped into the exam room.

The sight that met her eyes had her gulping back a silent gasp of shock. Luckily, the more professional side of her was able to contain the knee-jerk reaction. Quickly, though, she gathered herself together, her mind working overtime about how to deal with this shameful situation in a dignified manner.

Patsy Hubert, a fairly new patient in her mid-twenties, lay sprawled out on the exam table in the skimpiest and most provocative underwear Lyssa had ever seen. The woman was reaching for the T-shirt she'd tossed onto a nearby chair.

Lyssa turned her back, giving the patient a bit of privacy to dress. She spent several seconds focusing on the laptop, clicking the key that would save the electronic medical file, but her annoyance built with every second.

"Ms. Hubert," Lyssa said, unable to quell her tongue any longer, "I thought you came in to see the doctor about a sprained ankle?"

"I did."

Turning around, the closed laptop tucked under her arm, Lyssa pinned the woman with a sharp look. "Can you tell me why you felt it necessary to undress?"

The woman's eyes refused to meet hers. "W-well... I wasn't sure what to do. I thought maybe Dakota would like to—"

"Dr. Makwa," Lyssa interrupted rudely, incensed that the woman referred to her boss in so intimate a fashion, "sees ladies' undergarments all day long." No matter how hard Lyssa tried, she couldn't keep the anger out of her tone. She was livid on Dakota's behalf... because... well, just because the patient's intentions were so utterly and obnoxiously obvious. Dakota's spiritual beliefs might keep him from putting this woman in her place, but Lyssa didn't suffer from that problem. Not at all.

"Did you really think he'd be impressed with your black lace thong?" She raised one eyebrow and let the corner of her mouth twist with the derision that raced through her veins like acid.

Patsy swung her long, shapely legs over the side of the exam table and shimmied into her formfitting trousers.

"I came here," the woman said, her haughtiness in direct contradiction to the evident embarrassment reddening her face, "to see Dr. Makwa. Not to get a lecture from Nurse Nancy."

"Lyssa," she corrected. "My name is Lyssa."

Oh, there was plenty more Lyssa would have liked to say, but she dared not. It wasn't her intention to lose any patients for Dr. Dakota's practice. Her only purpose was to stand up for him when he seemed so unwilling to do so for himself.

Slipping down from the table, Patsy then

wiggled first one foot and then the other into her fashionable wedged sandals.

"Looks to me as if your ankle is just fine," Lyssa observed. "No redness. No swelling. And you obviously have full range of motion with it."

The young woman offered her a smile that was as fake as a three-dollar bill.

"Amazing, isn't it?"

Restraining the tirade that was going on inside her was difficult, but Lyssa succeeded. Finally, she said, "There won't be a charge for today."

She realized that she'd said that several times this week alone.

"Good," Patsy quipped, "because he spent less than five seconds in here. He didn't even look at my ankle."

The woman reached for her purse.

"Ms. Hubert—" Lyssa kept her gaze steady and level "—I'm sure Dr. Makwa would appreciate it in the future if you didn't waste his time. We have patients with legitimate ailments who are having trouble getting appointments."

The woman glared at her hard before jerking open the door and sauntering from the room.

Lyssa sighed and went to Dr. Dakota's office and knocked.

"Come in."

The chair behind his desk was empty. Movement in the periphery of her vision had her head swiveling.

He looked angry as a bear. And just as wild.

Lord above, he was a sight to behold as he stood by the window. His green eyes flashed with fury, his whole body taut with it, in fact. Lyssa had to garner all her nerve to simply enter the office and close the door behind her.

"She's gone," she announced. "Her ankle is fine, as I'm sure you saw."

Without looking at her, he said, "I saw more than I ever wanted to."

She moistened her dry lips, not quite knowing how to respond. Meaning only to calm him, she offered, "I suggested that she not waste your time in the future."

He looked as if he was about to implode. His agitated gaze was lighting on this and that, and Lyssa knew he wasn't seeing a thing. Finally, he turned to face her.

"That woman was all but naked!"

Distress was too mild a word to describe his state.

"Why weren't you in there with me? If patients disrobe, I need an assistant. This holds especially true with female patients these days. You know that."

The censure that dripped from his question took Lyssa aback.

"I'm sorry. She was seeing you for a twisted ankle. I didn't think you'd need me. There's only one of me around here and enough tasks for three people." Lyssa hated feeling the need to explain her actions. She couldn't bear feeling guilty for something she hadn't foreseen. She'd had enough of that in her past. "I assure you, Dr. Dakota, the patient was fully clothed when I came to fetch you. How was I to know she planned to give you a lingerie fashion show?"

In Lyssa's mind, the doctor's attack was unfair; however, her explanation hadn't seemed to abate his anger in the least.

He couldn't honestly hold her accountable for this fiasco, she realized suddenly. And if she thought back over the past few seconds, he hadn't actually blamed her for what happened. But, still, the pent-up fury in his gaze unsettled her. He was merely venting his frustration, she had to remember. Hadn't he told her that his Native American upbringing kept him from conveying his feelings in a way that might humiliate or offend another?

Seconds passed and Dr. Dakota's agitation continued to bubble like a pot of water on a heating element.

"This cannot go on," he said, the words fairly bursting from him. "My professional reputation could be in jeopardy. If one of those women were to become disgruntled or peeved by the fact that I'm not responding to her... her... *feminine wiles*, why, who knows what she might say, or what kind of accusations she might invent, or what could happen if..."

He just shook his head as the rest of his thought withered away, his hand worrying over his jaw.

"It's true," she found herself agreeing. "Hell hath no fury like a woman scorned. There can be a lot of truth in that. I get it."

"I could find myself in terrible trouble." He sighed, and then he leveled his gaze on her.

What she saw there wasn't blame, really. More

an expression of hurt. A mild reproach that told Lyssa he felt she could have helped him out of this days ago if she had chosen to... but she hadn't.

He hadn't uttered those words. He hadn't had to. It was all right there. In his wounded countenance.

"Dr. Dakota, I have good, solid reasons for not accepting your plan," she felt compelled to express. "You *have* to believe me."

"Oh?" His dark eyebrows rose a fraction. "And, tell me, Lyssa, are your reasons as good and as solid as the reasons I have for needing to stay away from those women who seem hell-bent on hunting me down and snaring me like I'm some kind of animal in the woods?"

In that instant she realized she couldn't answer his question. Because he hadn't explained his reasons to her. But now she knew without a doubt he intended to.

"Those women don't know me," he said. "They have no idea what I think or who I am. They might feel some kind of shallow sexual attraction, but that's all they feel. They want a trophy, Lyssa. And I've been there. I've done that. And I'll be damned if I'm getting trapped into that again."

Lyssa was relieved that she'd closed the door of

the office. Dakota didn't need anyone overhearing his tirade, although as worked up as he was at the moment, she doubted he cared one way or the other.

"It's not a pretty story," he told her. "I've been used. By a woman I loved. By a woman I thought loved me. Rose Marie Fletcher was the chief of surgery. The youngest woman to make chief at the small university hospital in Chicago where I studied. She was ambitious." His long hair fell over his shoulder when he turned his head. Softly, he added, "If only I'd caught on to the magnitude of her ambition, I may have saved myself some pain."

He paused a moment, and Lyssa saw that he didn't seem to be in this office any longer. He was someplace else. Someplace in the past.

"I was the only Native American in my graduating class," he continued. "That should have been a clue, I guess. But it wasn't one I picked up on." He drew his top lip between his teeth for a second, looking at a spot on the carpet between his feet. "You see, Rose Marie was beautiful. And she was smart. She was older than I was by nearly twelve years. But that hadn't mattered to me. I'd thought we were in love."

With unreserved disbelief, he murmured, "I changed every hope and dream I'd ever had for that woman."

He looked tired, as if pulling this memory up from the depths of his mind exhausted him. He leaned against his desk, hitching one hip onto the top of it. As for herself, she couldn't seem to move a muscle, so spellbound was she by his explanation.

"All I ever wanted to do was become a doctor and practice medicine here on the rez. Help the people of my tribe, my family, live healthy lives. But I turned away from that, turned away from the needs of the people on the rez because Rose Marie pushed and maneuvered and manipulated until her desire of our practicing together at some huge, prestigious institution somehow became my desire too."

The self-reproach he leveled on himself was more than Lyssa could bear. Without thinking, she whispered, "You loved her. You were trying to make her happy. That's what couples who love each other do."

"She didn't love me," he said plainly. "Oh, she married me. She took my name and used it for all it was worth. But her plans had nothing whatsoever to do with love."

Bewilderment knit Lyssa's forehead into a deep frown that she didn't bother to hide.

"One day," he said, "I overheard her bragging to a group of her peers. She'd accepted a phenomenal job offer... and she credited the real live Indian she'd caught with acquiring it. The man whose minority status opened doors for her that wouldn't normally be opened."

Lyssa sucked in a slow, deep breath. "Your wife used affirmative action to procure a position for herself? Even though she wasn't a minority? But... how?"

"Hospitals often hire husband-wife teams to practice. Being married to a Native American—"

"Hoisted her up the ladder of success," Lyssa sadly finished for him.

He was silent, his gaze steady.

Finally, he said, "I was devastated, Lyssa. I discovered that my wife was cold and calculating. The woman I loved was so compelled to control her own destiny that she'd use whatever means were at hand to get her where she wanted to go."

"Oh, Dakota," Lyssa breathed, "I'm so sorry."

The intimate manner in which she'd addressed her boss brought her up short. But judging from his preoccupation with the past, she doubted he'd even heard her. Then he lifted his chin and she saw gratitude shining in his eyes.

His jaw tightened. "What makes the situation even worse is that my mother had the same kind of deceitful character."

Lyssa's body tensed. What on earth had his mother done to bring about that kind of judgment from her son? But now wasn't the time to ask him to elaborate.

"I left Rose Marie," he told Lyssa. "Returned to Misty Glen just last year. I've been practicing here ever since... trying to build my original dream."

Touched by Dakota's story of betrayal, Lyssa moved across the room and positioned herself next to him, the desktop supporting her weight too. Their bodies weren't touching, but she was close enough, she felt, to offer him some sense of comfort.

"It's a nice dream," she said, hoping to encourage him. "Your practice is growing every day. Patients are coming, not just from the reservation, but also from nearby towns, to see you."

"Yes, but it's like a house of cards, Lyssa. One good puff of air—in the form of a scandal or malicious gossip or an indecent accusation—and it'll all come tumbling down." His eyes grew intense as he cast her a sidelong glance. He swallowed. His tone became as supple as velvet as he said, "But you could help me, Lyssa."

She groaned. "You're not going to start talking marriage again, are you? But what about love, Dr. Dakota? What about participating in a fulfilling lifelong relationship? You could have that, you know."

There was disdain in his tone as he said, "Believe me. Those things are highly overrated. I'm sure you've come to the same conclusion."

Lyssa sighed, smoothing restless fingers over her hair. Finally, she let her palm fall to slap her thigh. "You know I'm not using my married name at the moment."

"I've suspected it."

"Palmer is my grandmother's maiden name."

He just nodded.

"I'm telling you," she stressed, "there are good reasons why I shouldn't marry you."

"And I ask you again," he said, "can they match mine for needing to get married? My career could be on the line. Everything I'm working toward could be gone in a flash. You said it yourself, hell hath no fury..." He let the rest of his thought fade.

Her shoulders drooped. "Dr. Dakota, I don't want you any more involved in my life than you already are. My ex..." Anxiety had her shaking her head. "He comes from a powerful family. If he found out that Tori took me in, he'd have her B&B closed down. He could do it."

She lifted her hand. "And you? If he discovered that you gave me a job... if he found out that you helped me in any way, well, let's just say I've known what kind of trouble he can cause. I refuse to let him hurt you."

"Why don't you let me worry about me?"

The calm strength emanating from Dakota was more than a little impressive. Lyssa found herself wanting to soak it in, leach some of it from him. He seemed so self-assured and she loved that about him. She'd have liked to bare her soul to him, to tell him everything about her past, everything about her wretched ex-husband. Entrust him with every miserable mistake she'd made. But there was a small, frightened voice in her head that warned her against fully revealing herself to anyone. She'd been too hurt in the past.

"He could do more damage to your reputation than any of those predatory women you're worried about." Yet, even as she spoke the words, she could feel her resolve weakening. "Just by hiring me, you're in danger of his retaliation. If we were to—"

He pushed himself from the desk and he took her hands in his. "Like I said... let me worry about me." His expression sobered. "Is it possible, Lyssa, that all this power you think your ex has is in your mind? No one man can have that much authority over others. Not unless they allow it."

If anyone else had said those words, they might have sounded insulting. But Dakota hadn't meant them to harm. Only to enlighten. She realized that immediately.

"Maybe you're right," she said, her voice a mere whisper.

But as she thought about her life back in California, as she thought about all the guilt she'd been made to shoulder, as she thought about

Rodney and how childish and mean-spirited he had been, how determined he was to possess, to control, and how willing she'd been to be possessed and controlled...

Dark clouds gathered, and Lyssa shoved her way out of them.

"Besides," Dakota said, "if your ex-husband is as bad as you say, maybe what you need is a warrior—"

Then he did the most extraordinary thing. He placed the flat of his hand gently and protectively against her rounded tummy.

"Maybe what you both need is someone who'll stand by you," he said, his promise whisper soft, "through anything."

Hot tears welled up to scorch her eyeballs and she thought her heart would melt.

At first, she'd thought the situation he wanted to escape was silly; there would always be man-hungry women looking to capture a mate. But after hearing Dakota's tale of betrayal, she could understand why he wanted to steer clear of women who wanted him for the wrong reasons. However, in order to procure that protection for himself, he was willing to promise to stand by her, to defend her and her baby from an enemy he didn't even know. An enemy she knew to be formidable, even though Dakota might not believe it.

Maybe he was right, a tiny voice intoned. Maybe she did need a warrior. For her baby. For herself.

For the first time since fleeing California, Lyssa felt her dread lighten a bit.

"Okay." That one little word came out sounding like the croak of a frog even though the tension in her shoulders relaxed. "Let's do it, Dr. Dakota," she told him. "Let's get married."

Gratitude darkened his green gaze and he squeezed her hands in his. "So now can you drop the 'doctor'?"

CHAPTER THREE

———

"For every man there is a woman."

The rich timbre of the elderly shaman's voice sent a shiver coursing down the full length of Lyssa's spine. Although she stood close enough to her husband-to-be to sense the mass of him, feel his warmth, smell his intoxicating cologne, her wide-eyed gaze was trained on Dakota's grandfather. The man's face was lined with deep crevices, evidence that Shaman Grayson Makwa had lived a life filled with profound emotion.

"And he will know her," Grayson continued, "for she will touch his heart like no other. Every man must patiently wait for his Woman of the Heart."

———

Beside her, Dakota shifted his weight. But when she darted a quick look at him, he settled, his profile set with a firm resolve that made Lyssa nervous. What was going through his mind? Had he decided that maybe they were making a mistake? If so, she wished beyond reason that he'd speak up before it was too late. However, the thought was whisked right out of her head when the old shaman began to recite what he'd called the Wedding Prayer.

The Algonquian words had a lyrical rhythm that stirred her heart. She felt her anxiety begin to dissolve, and for the first time since the simple ceremony had begun, she smiled. Although she couldn't understand a single word he said, Lyssa knew Dakota's grandfather was petitioning The Great Spirit on her and Dakota's behalf.

Grayson wore an elaborate ceremonial headdress decorated in what looked to be a thousand pristine white feathers. Tassels heavy with polished stone beads hung from his temple regions and intricate stitching adorned the leather strip that swathed his forehead. There was no telling how many hours of painstaking labor had gone into the making of the beautiful headdress.

His tunic and trousers were made of animal hide, ornamented with more bead-work, and plain, unadorned moccasins covered his feet.

Flames danced and licked greedily at the large chunks of wood stacked on the bonfire. A hazy smoke wafted into the twilit sky, lending a true ethereal quality to the night.

Lyssa remembered when she'd wed Rodney, a day filled with stiff lace and sharp-edged diamonds, stretch limousines and white roses, pomp and circumstance... and strangers galore. Nearly five hundred people had packed the pews of the mega-church, many of whom she'd never met before—or after—that infamous day.

This simple yet oh-so-intimate ceremony was a direct contrast to that experience. Besides herself, Dakota and Grayson, there were only five other people in attendance. Tori Landing had happily agreed to act as Lyssa's maid of honor. Dakota's brother, Mat, Sheriff of Misty Glen Reservation was standing in as best man. Mat's fiancé, Julie, was seated with her brother Brian on her left and Mat's daughter Grace on her right. Julie and Mat had recently become an item, and it seemed as if the four of them had already settled into a happy family unit. The adoration in Julie's eyes as she looked at Mat really made Lyssa think.

People were supposed to marry for love. And she and Dakota were completely ignoring convention. They were laughing in the face of fate... marrying out of convenience. Would this disrespect of the sanctity of marriage get them into trouble? Lyssa hoped not. She had made enough mistakes in her life. And she had more than her share of responsibility to deal with already. Unwittingly, her hand slipped down over her tummy.

"Bless this union—" Grayson's arms lifted heavenward as he boldly made his plea toward the heavens "—and be with Dakota and Lyssa during every step of their new journey together."

He then took what looked to be a goblet cut of crude stone and set it in front of him. Into it he poured powder from a small drawstring pouch that he'd carried on a tether around his waist. He looked at Lyssa.

"This," he told her, "represents your past."

He poured in another small measure of powder and lifted his dark and somber gaze to Dakota's face.

"This represents your past."

56

Grayson then set aside the pouch and took up the goblet into both his hands. For a long moment, he held it up toward the sky, and then with a quick flick of his wrist, he tossed the powder into the fire in a manner that clearly demonstrated he'd done this many times before. Thick smoke billowed heavenward, and once the air cleared, Grayson's craggy face eased into a smile. "For the two of you, there is no yesterday. Only today. And many tomorrows."

The simplicity contained in that small act of symbolism brought tears to Lyssa's eyes. Oh, if only it were that easy to incinerate past failures. She'd experienced so many. So very many.

With one palm now firmly pressed against the swell of her pregnant belly, she felt emotion wallop her. She was determined that her child would not suffer for the blunders she had made. Surreptitiously, she snuck a quick glance at Dakota. He'd told her about his previous marriage. He saw it as a terrible mistake. He, too, must be wishing the same thing as she—that the errors of life could be burnt to meaningless ash with one mere toss of powder into flame.

Like some black cloud sliding down from the

universe above, guilt descended upon her, glutinous and smothering. Dakota had confessed to her about his past. He'd been honest and forthright about his first marriage. And she? Well, she had chosen to keep most of her secrets to herself.

She felt badly about that. But it really couldn't be helped. Dakota would have wanted nothing to do with her if he knew the entire truth about her life. About her past.

The old man had begun to softly chant, his shoulders lifting and falling gently with the beat of his ancient ceremonial song. It was lovely, and Lyssa let go of all the dire emotions in her and allowed herself to be enveloped in the poignancy of the moment. Finally, Grayson lowered his arms, looked at each of them in turn. Softly, he pronounced, "You are husband and wife."

For several heartbeats, a distinctive and awkward silence pulsed in the air. Neither Lyssa nor Dakota moved a muscle. The few wedding guests seemed to be breathless, waiting. Finally, the shaman chuckled.

"It is customary," Grayson said to the newlywed couple, "for the groom to kiss his bride."

Dakota's tone was hushed as he replied, "Of course."

The hue of his gaze was dark when he turned and leveled it on her, the emotion shadowed there unreadable, and Lyssa felt panic well in her chest. He leaned toward her, and tightening her grip on her small wildflower bouquet, she instinctively closed her eyes, her heart pounding against her ribs.

She had fantasized about his kiss. From the first day she'd gone to work in Dakota's office, she'd wondered what his mouth would feel like on her own. Wondered what his lips would taste like. Had even found herself daydreaming about it. She hadn't wanted to. She'd fought against the sensual speculations that had churned her thoughts, but they'd returned, again and again.

Well, now she was about to discover—

The warmth of his wide, velvet mouth pressed oh-too-fleetingly against hers.

And Lyssa found herself still standing there with her eyelids closed after he'd pulled away. She blinked. Inhaled. Recognized the emotion jolting through her as disappointment. She tamped down the sudden embarrassment of realizing that Dakota

59

had already turned from her. A strange awkwardness smacked her like an open palm against tender skin.

Grayson's coffee-colored eyes softened as her gaze found his.

"My daughter," he crooned, reaching out and taking her cheeks between his gnarled fingers, "welcome to the Makwa family. If you need me, I am here for you. Anytime of the day or night."

The warmth and total embrace emanating in his greeting made Lyssa's eyes well with unexpected tears. Never in her life had she been made to feel so accepted.

"Thank you." But her voice was barely audible, so tangled was it with chaotic emotion.

Grayson reached out for his grandson. "You know that I love you, my son. And want for you only happiness."

"Yes, Grandfather," Dakota said. "And I love you. With all my heart."

The exchange between the men should have been moving, but Lyssa couldn't help but notice an odd strain in her new husband's words, nor could she miss the tension manifested on his handsome face.

Again, she wondered if he'd changed his mind. If he'd decided that marrying her wasn't a good idea after all, yet hadn't spoken up in time to put a stop to the ceremony. Dread knotted Lyssa's insides. She disliked the idea that Dakota might come to see her as just one more mistake he'd made in his life.

Tori hugged Lyssa to her, emotion shining in her blue eyes. "I'm so happy for you," she whispered. The woman fairly shivered with joy as she pressed her cheek to Lyssa's.

Swiveling her head, Lyssa lifted her gaze just in time to see Dakota take his brother's proffered hand.

"I just hope you know what you're doing," Mat murmured.

The man's words were grave with gentle warning and his hawkishly handsome features were drawn. Lyssa couldn't miss the implication that, in his opinion, this union didn't have the slightest chance of succeeding.

"Mat!" Julie's light laugh didn't hide the censure she obviously intended. "Is that any way to congratulate your brother?" Without waiting for an answer, she threw her arms around Dakota's neck.

"No matter what your brother has to say, I wish you all the best, Dakota."

"Thanks, Julie," he said. "Mat's just a little grumpy because he couldn't talk me out of this. He's been quite candid about his opinion that Lyssa and I are making a mistake. I respect that." Dakota lifted one shoulder in a small shrug. "And he might be right—could be I'm going to need all the good wishes I can get."

The leaden feeling in Lyssa's stomach magnified. Oh, he was sorry. That realization was becoming clearer by the moment.

Evidently feeling that his position needed some backing, Mat said, "Well, you've got to admit that you two hardly know each other. You should have followed after my example—" he hugged Julie to him "—and waited a while. Get to know each other first, like me and Julie. Our wedding is set for Christmas—"

"And I say," Julie cut him off with a bright smile, her green gaze glittering, "that now isn't the time for this discussion. In fact, waiting is no longer an option for Dakota and Lyssa, dear heart. In case you missed it, they have just been pronounced husband and wife. Right now, you should be hugging your new sister-in-law."

Good manners were enough to have Mat looking contrite. "I'm sorry, Lyssa," he said before giving her a quick peck on the cheek. "I didn't mean to put a damper on things."

Out of the corner of her eye, Lyssa saw young Grace surreptitiously tug at the hem of Brian's dark suit jacket.

"Lyssa's going to have a baby," the six-year-old astutely observed.

"She is," Brian remarked, nodding.

Grace's pert nose wrinkled as she pondered the implications. Then she said, "I thought only married people could have babies."

Sudden anxiety tightened in Lyssa's stomach. How could the teen ever explain this complicated situation in a manner the child could comprehend? How on earth could Brian even understand it all?

But the boy only shrugged and said, "Well, they *are* married... now."

Grace seemed to take the answer in stride. "Oh," she said, nodding in agreement. "I guess you're right."

Mat leaned close to Lyssa's ear. "I'm sorry about

that, too." He indicated his daughter with a tip of his head.

Lyssa attempted a smile, but her muscles felt wooden. "It's okay. She's so young. And I know that you're only looking out for your brother's best interests."

He paused a moment, just studying her face. His hands were warm as they squeezed hers gently. "Welcome to the family. I mean that."

It was impossible not to know that this man had been against Dakota's marrying her, but his welcome seemed genuine. At that moment, Lyssa realized that Mat would never leave her in doubt as to where she stood with him. She could trust that he'd always make his thoughts and opinions perfectly clear.

She only wished she could say the same about Dakota.

He'd seemed so adamant about their getting married. Had said that this marriage would be the answer to all their problems, hers and his. Yet here he was, seemingly torn and tense about the situation—now that it was too late to do anything to avert it.

Julie's palms slid over Lyssa's shoulders. Her eyes

twinkled. "Never mind Mat," Julie told her. "He's just too serious for his own good sometimes." She smiled then, wide and welcoming. "Congratulations."

"Thank you," Lyssa breathed as the woman hugged her tightly.

Julie whispered, "Before you know it, we'll be sisters-in-law, you and I. We'll be great friends. I can just feel it."

Yes, Mat and Julie would marry at Christmas, but would Dakota and Lyssa still be together then, Lyssa wondered. Would she still be living on Misty Glen Reservation? Or would her past have caught up with her? Forced her to flee to a new and different place?

"We've got a lot to do," Dakota said to the group at large.

Lyssa realized that he was ready to make his exit.

"Oh, no," Julie said. "You're not taking Lyssa anywhere until she has a chance to toss that bouquet to the single ladies."

Remembering the huge spray of white roses she'd carried when she'd wed Rodney, Lyssa now looked down at the small bunch of wildflowers that Grayson had so thoughtfully provided for her today when she'd arrived. The flowers were so lovely that she hated to part with them; however, it was clear that Julie was hankering after the chance to catch the bouquet and thereby seal her fate as the next unattached female who would catch herself a husband.

"Okay," Lyssa said to Julie and Tori. "Get ready."

She positioned herself about ten feet in front of them, turned her back, counted to three and tossed the bouquet up and over her head toward the women.

Laughter echoed in the air, and the squeals of surprise had Lyssa twisting on her heel.

There, with her eyes wide with utter astonishment, stood Tori Landing holding the colorful wildflowers.

~oOo~

Dakota hadn't said a word since they left the ceremony, and Lyssa felt her nerves were coiled as tight as an overwound clock spring. A frown marred Dakota's handsome face, and with every second that ticked by, it seemed that his mood grew darker. Finally, Lyssa could take it no longer.

"Okay," she blurted, her voice echoing against the windows of the car, "I'm sorry. I'm sorry that you're sorry. I'm sure we can get this marriage annulled. All we have to do is—"

"What?"

The surprise contained in that tiny query, in Dakota's green gaze when he shot a glance her way, startled her into silence.

"What are you talking about?" he asked when she didn't answer him immediately. "We're not going to have our marriage annulled." Then a thought seemed to dawn on him. "Is that what you want?"

He looked at her, then looked at the roadway ahead. However, obvious agitation had him casting his gaze on her again as he awaited her answer and Lyssa realized that there were probably safer places to have this conversation than in a moving vehicle.

Confusion made her thoughts go haywire. "Well... no," she told him. "B-but I thought... you've been so quiet. Sullen, even. And after hearing what Mat had to say... well, I thought you may have changed your mind."

"You can't listen to Mat." Dakota shook his head. "Like Julie said, the man's too serious for his own good. Our marriage was no mistake. This is the answer to my prayers." He pitched her a soft look. "I hope it's the answer to yours, too."

His words should have set her mind at ease, but she was too perplexed for that.

"Then would you please tell me what's wrong?" she said. "You've been acting like a dark horse ever since your grandfather pronounced us man and wife." He sighed heavily. "It's my grandfather. Or rather, the ceremony he chose."

Lyssa thought about the shaman, his beautiful regalia, the lovely prayers sung in his native language.

"I thought it was wonderful." She tried to keep the wistfulness out of her tone. "It was warm. And intimate. So different from my first wedding, let me tell you. That fiasco was huge. And so cold that the ice sculpture could have lasted a week."

Dakota smiled over at her then. "Today was different from my first wedding, too," he murmured. "I got married in a courthouse. No family. No friends. That ceremony was small. But just like yours, it was pretty frosty." He chuckled. "And just like yours, it was a fiasco."

The scowl was gone from his face, and she felt

as if a great weight had been lifted off her. At least now she knew he didn't regret marrying her.

"Looks like we have something in common," she said. "First weddings that were—" she searched a proper description "—less than pleasant."

"Looks like it," he agreed.

She sat quietly for a moment, and then she asked, "What was it about the ceremony that bothered you? I thought your grandfather did a wonderful job." Before she even had time to think, she pointed out, "He called me the woman of your heart."

The corners of her mouth pulled back in a smile. The idea might be a little far-fetched and much too romantic, since she and Dakota had known each other such a short amount of time, yet Grayson had still touched a tender place inside her.

Instantly, Dakota's dark humor returned full force. "His mention of the legend was his way of prodding me."

"What legend? What are you talking about?"

"Many Native American tribes have stories and legends that deal with finding one's true love. Usually, they're told for the benefit of the female. Sort of like the Cinderella story. Or the tale of the knight in shining armor."

Lyssa remembered her own youth. Where she grew up, it was common knowledge that no knight, shining or otherwise, would ever show up for the rescue. So Lyssa had taken things into her own hands. And in doing so, she'd made a royal mess of her life!

"Well," Dakota continued, "the legend of the Woman of the Heart is told for the benefit of the young men of the tribe. We're told that each of us has a woman who was born just for us."

Lyssa spoke softly as she recited the shaman's words, "*And he will know her. For she will touch his heart like no other.*"

Warmth shot through her like a hot-tipped arrow. Gooseflesh rose on her arms, making her shiver. The notion was a lovely one. A little fanciful maybe, but terribly romantic nonetheless.

"It was what he tacked on at the end that upset me," Dakota said. "The part about a man patiently waiting for his woman."

"So your grandfather wasn't referring to me." She spoke slowly as she fit the pieces together. "You think he was being facetious. He was pointing out that I'm not the woman for you. That you should have waited for *her* rather than marry me."

Disappointment washed through her. She'd thought Grayson had been so friendly toward her. So unconditionally welcoming. When the shaman had called her the woman of Dakota's heart, Lyssa had taken that to mean that the old man thought she and his grandson were meant to be together—even though their union wasn't based on love—and that had touched her. Deeply.

This whole train of thought was silly, really. She had gone into this knowing there was no emotion involved. Her eyes had been open to the fact that this would be a marriage of convenience... a platonic merger... a sleep-in-separate-rooms business agreement between herself and Dakota.

So why did she feel like crying now that she'd discovered that Grayson Makwa's statements hadn't been meant as she'd originally taken them?

It was clear that Dakota didn't notice her disappointment. He was too wrapped up in his own thoughts.

"I suppose Grandfather is disturbed that we rushed into getting married," he said. "Obviously, he disapproves of what we're doing and why we're doing it. I've been divorced once. And I guess he sees you and I ending up the same way. I'm sure that's why he said what he said." After a moment, he blurted, "Well, he can disapprove all he wants. So can Mat, for that matter. The fact that they frown on what we've chosen to do means nothing to me."

Funny, Lyssa thought, how she had chosen to focus on the beautiful and heartrending aspects of the ceremony performed by the shaman—the lovely legend and the warm reception into the Makwa family—while Dakota had focused only on his family's disapproval.

He chose that moment to reach over and slide his fingers lightly over her thigh.

"We did what was right for us," he said, his tone louder than it needed to be. "That's all that matters."

She knew his touch was meant solely as reassurance. He meant to support, encourage, spur faith in the decisions they had made. However, the manner in which her body responded to the heat of his palm as it penetrated the thin fabric of her skirt was nothing short of overwhelming.

The weight of his hand set her emotions churning. Her heart pounded. Something deep inside her sprouted to life, curling, swirling, growing.

She wasn't completely naive. She'd been married. She'd felt sexual urges before. But the passion that Dakota sparked in her body, ignited in her blood, was so potent, so powerful that it swept all thought from her head.

She wanted him! In the most physical way possible. She wanted to taste his kiss. A real kiss. Not a sweet little peck like the one he'd given her at the ceremony. She wanted to feel his hands on her. She wanted to run her fingertips through his hair, experience the silky length of it against her skin. She wanted to touch his body.

Suddenly, it was absolutely impossible for her to draw a breath.

Lyssa knew he was waiting for her to agree with him. He was looking for the same kind of encouragement and support that he'd just offered her. He needed to hear that she was on his side in this, that the two of them were a team. No matter what the rest of the world thought about what they were doing or their motivation for doing it.

But she couldn't think, couldn't speak. All she could do was sit there next to him, wanting him, needing him, all the while being taunted by that small frantic voice ringing through her brain.

Girl, it warned, you are in some deep trouble.

CHAPTER FOUR

———

"Come in," Dakota called from his desk when he heard the knock on his office door.

Lyssa's golden-brown eyes were smiling when she entered.

"Hi," he said automatically. The mere sight of her had his shoulders relaxing, and he set aside his tablet.

"You've got a patient waiting in exam room one," she told him.

"Thanks." He was staring, he knew. But he couldn't help it.

The afternoon sunlight spilling in from the solitary window gave her hair a honey glow. She wore it up at the office, but at home she wore it down. That's how he liked it. Loose and free, tumbling soft around her shoulders.

Self-consciously, he glanced back down at the notes he'd been making on the patient's file. He shouldn't think about such things. However, over the past few days since they had married and Lyssa had moved in with him, those kinds of unbidden thoughts infiltrated his mind more and more frequently.

He realized she was still standing at the door. "I'll be right there."

Her luscious mouth pulled into a small grimace and her nose wrinkled across the bridge. Dakota was struck with the notion that she was just too delectable for decency.

"I think I'd better warn you." Her voice lowered as if she was about to confide some secret that she didn't want anyone else to hear. "It's Desiree Washington."

He groaned. His stomach knotted at the thought of dealing with the woman. "But she was just here last week. And she was healthy as a horse."

Lyssa chuckled, and he would have loved to dive headfirst into the pleasant sound of it. But right now it seemed he had a problem to face.

"I believe," she said lightly, "that Ms. Washington would be appalled by your analogy. However—" again her tone lowered conspiratorially "—she looks pretty healthy to me, too." Laughter bubbled up from Lyssa's throat again and she shook her head. "You've got to feel sorry for the poor woman. The only cure for her 'illness' would be a lustectomy."

A bark of laughter erupted from him before he was able to contain it. "I've never performed that procedure."

It was amazing that Lyssa seemed to be able to bring a ray of sunshine into a dismal situation. However, dread still lumped in his gut at the thought of going into the exam room.

Dakota was a competent doctor. An intelligent man. So why was it that the mere idea of dealing with the likes of Desiree Washington—or any other man-hungry woman—filled him with such alarm?

"Would you stop looking so defeated?"

Something in Lyssa's tone had his eyes lifting to hers.

"You've got a plan?" he asked, hearing the hope that heavily laced the edges of his question. He didn't care that he sounded desperate. He just wanted to stop feeling like a fat and juicy rabbit being pursued by ravenous wolves.

"Oh," she said, her gorgeous eyes twinkling with undisguised merriment, "I've got something better than a plan. I've got a wedding ring."

She grinned, lifting her left hand and wiggling her fingers for Dakota's benefit. He couldn't help but return a cockeyed grin of his own.

"Come on," she prompted, reaching out her hand to him. "It's time to let Ms. Washington know that hunting season for Dakota Makwa is over."

It was clear to Lyssa that, from the moment she and Dakota entered the exam room, the patient was thrown off kilter by the presence of the nurse. Lyssa immediately settled herself in a chair, laptop open and balanced on her knees, as she and the doctor had agreed to give the woman the benefit of the doubt just in case she might have a legitimate medical concern. However, it became apparent that the patient really was as healthy as that proverbial horse.

Desiree hemmed and hawed when Dakota asked her to describe her illness. She ended up talking about this and that, the general stresses of her life, never really detailing any viable symptoms, all the while shooting covert, yet telling, glances at Lyssa. If looks could kill, Lyssa highly suspected she'd have been a goner for sure.

Oh, this woman was good. The smile she gifted Dakota was coy and enticing. Her fingers trailed up to toy with her hair often. And she had a way of dipping her chin so that she was forced to look up at him through lowered lashes. Desiree had the art of flirting down to a well-rehearsed science. No wonder Dakota had felt threatened by her. She clearly saw him as ready prey—and she'd come loaded with her best ammunition.

While watching the scene unfold, some strange emotions began to churn inside Lyssa. Protective feelings, that was certain. She'd expected those. Protecting Dakota from the likes of Desiree Washington was the very reason she was here. The very reason she'd married him. But something else was stewing in her gut, as well. Something she couldn't quite put a name to.

Finally, Desiree turned her full attention on Lyssa, nailing her with a withering look as she huffed out a haughty sigh.

"My problem is very private," the woman said. "I was hoping to see the doctor alone." Then she turned pleading eyes on Dakota, batting them for good measure as she asked, "Do you think that would be possible?"

The nameless substance bubbling down deep rose up in Lyssa, inky and viscous. This woman needed taking down a peg or two, and Lyssa would have loved nothing more than to do just that. However, she remembered that treating people with dignity and respect was important to Dakota.

Oh, she planned on letting Desiree have it. She'd just have to choose her words with care, is all.

Everyone knew that bad-tasting medicine always went down easier with a bit of sugar, so Lyssa forced herself to smile sweetly as she informed Desiree, "We have a new policy in the office. A nurse will always be present while the doctor is with his patients. It's a guideline being set in lots of medical offices these days. I'm sure you can understand. And it's for everyone's benefit, the patient's as well as the doctor's."

With each sentence Lyssa spoke, Desiree's spine seemed to grow straighter, her expression turning darker, her eyes narrowing.

Was that a challenge she saw reflected in the woman's gaze? Lyssa wondered. Could it be possible that Desiree Washington was that dull-witted? Could she really believe that she could get to Dakota even after being told openly and plainly that it would no longer be possible for her to see the doctor alone in the office?

The questions stirred Lyssa's ire. What she'd like to have done was smack some sense into Desiree's foolish head. However, Lyssa forced another smile onto her mouth, this one filled with joy. She released a small ring of elated laughter.

"And I promise you," Lyssa said with utter sincerity, "this new policy is based solely on our determination to give our patients the best and most professional care available. And the change has absolutely nothing to do with the fact that Dr. Makwa and I were married this past weekend."

Desiree's face went pale and she stammered, "M-m-m—"

"Married!" Lyssa supplied, grinning now from ear to ear. "Isn't it wonderful?"

"B-but you've only been working in the office—"

"Such a short time, I know." Lyssa's gaze lit with

excitement. This was too much fun. "Isn't love just the most mysterious and amazing thing?"

Desiree took that moment to direct her attention to Dakota. So did Lyssa.

One look at the man and Lyssa knew she was in trouble. He was obviously bowled over by her performance. He stood there, his square jaw slightly slackened, his green eyes wide.

Oh, Lord above, if he was given the chance to speak, who knew what might come out of his mouth? Lyssa had to do something. Quick.

She stood, set the laptop onto the counter and moved over next to Dakota. She curled her fingers possessively over his forearm and then turned to look once again at Desiree. The woman seemed to be not only recouping from the news but also to be regrouping as well.

In that nanosecond, Lyssa became determined that Desiree was going to leave this office today knowing that Dakota was taken. That he was no longer available. To her or anyone else.

"We just couldn't be happier," Lyssa crooned. She tipped her face up to Dakota. "Could we, darling?"

He opened his mouth to speak, and she was

overcome with sudden panic. In an attempt to keep him silent, she reached up on tiptoe and—

Kissed him!

She pressed her slightly parted lips to his, curled her fingers over his muscled shoulder, all the while frantic over how he'd react to her brazen behavior.

He tasted fiery sweet, and current zipped through her entire body. Heat flushed across every inch of her skin. His hands splayed on her back and she soon found herself pulled up tight against him.

The warm scent of him enveloped her like a soft and sensual cloak, and she relaxed into the delicious haze that danced and swirled around them. She was light-headed and woozy. Blood whooshed through her ears at such a rate that she became deaf to the sounds of the outside world. She felt isolated, as if she and Dakota were the only two people on earth.

The errant thought moaned through her mind that she didn't want this moment to end... *ever*. But the kiss had to end. Because they weren't the only two people on earth. They weren't even the only two people in the small examination room.

When the two of them parted, Lyssa was aware of the dull jab of sadness that cut through her. Had that soft and contented sigh really been uttered from her lips?

She paused a moment, attempting to regain her equilibrium, and then she lifted her gaze to his. The expression in his moss-green eyes, in the honed angles of his handsome face, was unreadable. One breathless heartbeat passed. Then a second. And a third.

Lyssa's hazy brain cleared like a morning fog burned off by the rising sun. The sound of paper crinkling behind her made Lyssa's eyes widen a bit. Desiree Washington remained seated on the exam table, shifting, and clearly disgusted with the newlyweds' display of affection.

Spinning to face the woman, Lyssa hoped the smile on her face didn't slip out of position. But her knees felt weak and she wasn't sure she could stand on her own for very long.

Desiree's mouth flattened into a straight slash. Disapproval evident in the tight muscles of her face. "I don't like this new policy change," she said, putting ugly emphasis on the last two words. She slid herself off the table. "I'm afraid I'm going to have to find myself a new doctor."

Losing Dakota a patient hadn't been Lyssa's

intention, but she'd be lying if she said she would be sorry to see the last of the woman.

"If you'll let our office know the name of your new physician," Lyssa offered, "we'll forward your records right away."

The woman's expression contracted with contempt, but she picked up her purse and left without saying another word to either of them.

Alone with Dakota, Lyssa's legs grew shakier. In fact, they seemed to be turning to gelatinous rubber. She couldn't look at him, and awkwardness pulsed in the close confines of the small room. Finally, she garnered enough nerve to lift her eyes to his. His sexy mouth was cocked into a grin that was so charming Lyssa felt the urge to curl her toes right through the soles of her shoes.

"You called me darling."

Mortification solidified in her stomach and she groaned. "I *know*. It sounded so hokey, didn't it?"

Dakota's shoulder lifted and then fell. "I don't know about hokey, but that little pet name—and that kiss—sure did the trick with Desiree. You're quite the actress, Lyssa."

Something strange twinkled in his eyes, and she

didn't know whether to feel embarrassed or pleased.

Hesitantly, she found herself saying, "I-I'm sorry. I shouldn't have—"

"Oh, no," he rushed to cut her off. "Don't you dare be sorry." He picked up the laptop she'd set on the counter and tucked it beneath his arm. "This turned out to be a pretty enjoyable afternoon. So enjoyable, in fact, that I'm sort of looking forward to having some of my other man-hunting patients come in for a visit."

He slipped out the door then, leaving her all alone.

Her emotions were in a jumble as she tried to decipher all that had happened, all that her boss—her husband—had said. All that he'd implied.

Her knees continued to tremble, and Lyssa was forced to ease herself down into the chair. She hadn't planned on being unable to contain her desire for Dakota. And she certainly hadn't imagined that he might desire her.

"Silly woman," she whispered aloud.

He didn't desire her. How could he? She was round as a basketball with this baby. She was running from a bad relationship. Hiding from an ex-husband she feared. How could a man find any of that desirable?

But she couldn't get out of her mind the image of that sensuous grin on Dakota's face. Of that suggestive glitter in his green eyes.

And all she could do was sit there, gulp in head-clearing air, and wonder.

~oOo~

She was avoiding him. Dakota didn't have a single doubt about it. Lyssa had taken to staying late at the office in order to escape spending time with him in the evenings.

He grinned as he dipped the brush into the bucket of pastel paint.

The scene in the exam room this past week continued to run through his head. He'd been bowled over at the time by Lyssa's surprising self-assuredness. What sass! She'd boldly announced her claim on him as his new wife and then approached him so intimately. She'd kissed him right there in front of Desiree Washington.

His chuckle echoed off the bare walls of the freshly painted room and he shook his head in amazement. Lyssa was remarkable. This wasn't the first time he'd come to that conclusion. And he had an idea it wouldn't be the last, either.

She just had a way about her. A special... way.

He had no other words to describe her.

You're attracted to her, a small voice accused from the back of his brain.

A slight scowl drew his eyebrows together. What he was feeling was not attraction. He liked Lyssa, sure. But he refused to allow his feelings to grow to anything more than the mere affection that currently flooded his being when he thought of her.

She's a gorgeous woman, the voice mocked. You'll never resist those striking golden-brown eyes of hers. If given the chance, you'd happily surrender once again to her luscious-tasting lips.

His head shook in a firm, dissenting response. The jerky motion sent a drip of paint spattering on the carpet. He heaved a noisy exhalation of disgust and immediately grabbed for the wet cloth he had on hand for just such messes.

As he dabbed at the spot, Dakota gave himself a good talking-to.

"You are not interested in a relationship here,"

he muttered, his words grating with resolve. "It doesn't matter that she's beautiful. It doesn't matter that her eyes flash with quick wit. It doesn't matter that her mouth tastes like sweet wine."

The deepest part of him stirred and warmth snaked through his body in languid, coiling tendrils. Dakota closed his eyes, wanting to shun the glorious agony winding through him, yet also wanting to savor it, get lost in it. Finally, he let out a growl, tossing the rag aside, clearing his mind and dipping his brush again into the pale green paint.

Why don't you just admit it? The question reverberated jeeringly. You're attracted to her.

Desperately.

"I am not!"

So why had he spent the last three evenings preparing this surprise for her? Why had he gone out of his way to keep his work a secret in order to spring the project on her once it was finished?

Because she'd had a rough time of it, that was why. She was on the run. From what must have been a very bad situation. She could use a little joy. Those were the only reasons he was doing what he was doing.

He was determined not to get intimately

involved. Dakota had his fill of the hurt that came with loving relationships. He'd been betrayed. Rose Marie had taken the love he'd offered and twisted it up until it had become unrecognizable even to him. When Dakota had arrived home to Misty Glen, his emotions had been in such a state that he hadn't thought he'd even survive the experience.

And the betrayal he'd encountered involved another woman he'd loved, and it reached far back into his past. His mother had treated him treacherously. Her disloyalty continued to affect him every day of his life. Why, he was forced to confront it every single time he looked into a mirror....

The black cloud that descended on him was frightening in the dire emotion it carried along with it, so Dakota shoved and pushed his way out of it.

Focus on the work at hand, he told himself calmly.

And the work at hand was being done for the sole purpose of bringing a smile to the face of one extraordinary woman for whom Dakota merely felt a friendly affection.

He sighed with an easy satisfaction. With his motivation now clearly defined, he felt better.

After one last brush stroke, he stood and inspected his efforts, feeling both pleased with himself and certain that Lyssa was in for a grand surprise.

~oOo~

She was avoiding him. There was no doubt about that.

For the past three days, she'd spent hours reorganizing the office. She'd cleaned out the supply closet. She'd even figured out how to integrate phone numbers into the new texting system that would alert patients to the dates and times of their appointments.

Lyssa stifled a yawn. She was tired. She'd been on her feet all day, and the extra hours she was putting in during the evenings were taking their toll on her pregnant body. She looked at the clock on the wall.

If she could just stay for twenty more minutes, she could arrive at home and head straight for a hot bath. After that she could climb directly into bed, and there would be no need for her to have too much conversation with Dakota.

Ever since she'd instigated that kiss, her feelings had become nothing short of anarchic where her new husband was concerned. She found herself thinking about him constantly. He'd made it perfectly clear that he wasn't interested in becoming involved in a relationship. He'd been hurt, lied to, used in the past.

What on earth was wrong with her?

She'd just left a horrible relationship. She'd traveled clear across the country in order to find her freedom. In order to find herself. What was she doing yearning for another man?

Truth be told, the kind of yearning she felt for Dakota was different than anything she'd felt for Rodney.

It had been many months since she'd actually longed for a close bond with her ex. And thinking she could conjure up one with that mean-spirited man had been a mistake, especially since she'd married him under those now-regretful circumstances. Still, Rodney had made promises that had lured her into thinking things might be different.

So many promises...

Sadness threatened to tumble down on her, but she shrugged it off. She was through feeling badly over her first marriage. Granted, all those sour feelings were her own fault. But she was done with that, nonetheless.

Right now, she had to deal with her emotions regarding Dakota, or rather her physical responses to the man. She'd never been treated with the kind of gentleness and respect with which he treated her.

Her chin tipped up. Surely that was the root of her response to him. He was kind and caring. A wonderful man. Any woman would feel attracted to that. And she was dealing with a body raging with hormones. So it was no wonder that he triggered feelings in her—sensuous consequences to his kind overtures.

That was it, she decided. Now all she had to do was restrain herself.

A rude snort gushed from her lips, and she covered her grin with her fingers. Oh, if only it were as easy as it sounded. Now, avoiding Dakota altogether, that was something she was becoming adept at.

Rising from the desk chair, Lyssa shut down the

laptop, then crossed the room and flipped off the light. It was time to go home, take a bath, and crawl into bed.

Dakota's office sat right next to his home. In fact, the two structures were connected by a hallway. For the past two nights that Lyssa had come in, the house had been dark and quiet. But tonight there seemed to be lights on in every room.

Fearing that something was wrong, Lyssa went in search of Dakota, and she found him in the small laundry room just off the kitchen.

"Hello," he greeted brightly as he tucked the ironing board into the linen closet.

"Is everything all right?"

"Sure is. I'm just tidying up a bit. I was pressing some curtains."

"Pressing curtains?" Automatically, she glanced at her watch. He normally retired to his room pretty early. "But... isn't it awfully late for that?"

Excitement danced in his green eyes, and Lyssa found it so enchanting that she forced herself to look away.

"It's not that late," he told her. "I'm glad you're home. I've got a surprise for you."

Lyssa hated surprises. Surprises meant gifts.

And gifts meant that the giver was looking for something in return. During her marriage, she'd quickly come to realize that anytime she was given a present, she was expected to reciprocate a favor. And the payback was never pleasant.

Her hesitance must have tipped Dakota off regarding her uncertainty. He laughed.

"Come on now," he said. "It's a good surprise. I promise."

He took her hand and propelled her toward the back of the house.

His skin felt so warm against her own, his hold on her secure, and Lyssa was left wondering how any woman could give up a man like this once she'd captured his heart. *Poor Rose Marie*, the errant thought of Dakota's ex floated through Lyssa's mind, unbidden. The woman had been an idiot to let him go.

Dakota walked past his bedroom door, and then hers. He stopped at the third bedroom.

"Go ahead," he urged her softly. "Go in."

Lyssa looked at him, tentativeness making her feel quavery inside. Dakota was not Rodney, she silently reminded herself. Dakota was honorable.

He was kind. He wouldn't be looking for any kind of turnabout.

Slowly, she turned the doorknob and gently pushed open the door. Dakota reached around her and flicked on the light switch.

Lyssa inhaled audibly. And her heart melted.

"Oh, my," she breathed. "B-but—"

"You've never mentioned whether or not you know the sex of the baby," he said in a rush, nudging her farther inside the nursery. "So I opted for celery green and yellow. That'll work for a girl or a boy, don't you think?"

She couldn't answer. She couldn't think straight. Emotions swam and collided.

The freshly painted walls were green with white trim. Lemon-yellow curtains fluttered in the autumn breeze coming in through the window.

"A crib!" She moved to stand beside the bed, running her fingertips along the top of the railing. A colorful mobile hung at the head. The mattress was covered with a downy sheet, a fluffy teddy bear nestled in one corner. She glanced at the white rocking chair sitting next to the crib. "How did you do all this without my knowing?"

He grinned. "You've been awfully busy the past

few evenings." His smile broadened. "And so have I."

She picked up the furry brown teddy bear and hugged it to her chest. Her eyes blurred with hot tears.

"Hold on now. You're not going to cry on me, are you? I did all this to make you happy."

"I am happy."

His tone softened to a croon as he came up behind her, his hands sliding onto her shoulders. "So why the tears?"

"I don't know." She sniffed, then blurted, "I'm a pregnant woman," as if that could explain everything.

In reality, Lyssa had never been so moved, so stirred with... with...

She couldn't put a name to what she was feeling. No one had ever done something this wonderful for her. Ever.

Finally, she whispered, "Dakota, my baby's not due for five months. Do you really think I'll still be here then?"

She couldn't see his face, but sensed he was surprised by her question.

"I know we never talked about just how long our

marriage would last, but it never entered my head that you'd leave before the baby arrived."

She was quite shaky now, a condition she found herself in frequently when she was in Dakota's company. The man was always doing something or other that stole her breath away. Whether it was simply looking devastatingly handsome, or saying something kind and reassuring, or creating a nursery for her child, the man was just too wonderful for words.

As she stood by the lovely crib, he slipped his arms around her until he held her securely. He rested his chin on her shoulder and gently ruffled the teddy bear's fur.

"We had a deal," he told her. "You've helped me immensely. Women like Desiree Washington are much less of an issue in my life. And word has gotten around that I'm a married man now. My problems are well on their way to being solved."

He pulled her more securely against him and she didn't resist.

"Now," he whispered, "I think our goal is to see that the remainder of your pregnancy is as stress-free as possible."

Lyssa had never really been in love before, never

lost her heart to a man. She'd found herself married to her first husband for all the wrong reasons. And she'd thought—up until that very second, at least— that her marriage to Dakota had been based on some pretty mixed-up reasons, too.

But if she were to hazard a guess, she'd feel safe saying that if someone were to x-ray her chest right at this moment, it would be empty. And her heart? Well, her heart was in the palm of Dakota's hand.

CHAPTER FIVE

———

"What is that delicious smell?"

The appreciative tone of Dakota's voice made Lyssa smile. Ever since he'd surprised her with the nursery, she'd decided to do what she could to repay him. Over the past few days, she cleaned the house, did the shopping, and cooked nice dinners for him. These small offers of appreciation, she felt, were the least she could do. He'd given her so much. A job. A safe place to live. Compassion. Concern. Respect.

She wasn't motivated by feelings of obligation; in no way was this situation anything like what her ex had forced on her. No, she did these things because she wanted to do them. She enjoyed seeing Dakota's enthusiastic smile when he found his shirts had been freshly laundered and hung in his closet. She especially enjoyed hearing his compliments when they sat down to eat together each evening.

Lyssa had stopped the silly practice of avoiding Dakota. She'd realized that, since he had been honorable enough to tell her honestly that he wasn't interested in a relationship, she could be mature enough to respect that. The attraction she felt for him continued, but that didn't mean she had to act on those feelings.

She'd been so moved by what he'd done. The nursery had been an amazing surprise. An overwhelming gift. Even now just thinking about it made her go tingly all over.

"It's gumbo," she told him. "New Orleans style."

His eyes lit up. "Spicy?"

She grinned. "Very."

Their gazes caught and held. The air hummed and vibrated. Yet Lyssa made herself turn away from the moment. She focused her attention on lifting the pot lid and giving the contents a thorough stir.

She served the gumbo over steaming white rice.

Crusty bread and a nice sparkling grape juice rounded out the meal.

"This is wonderful," Dakota said. "Delicious."

A blush warmed her cheeks. "Thanks." She picked up her glass and took a sip.

"Your mother did a good job."

Lyssa nearly choked at the mention of her mother. "I beg your pardon?"

He chuckled, seemingly unaware of her strangled reaction. "I can image the two of you cooking marvelous dinners together as she taught you all about slicing, dicing, and secret spices."

Now it was her turn to laugh, but hers held a hint of nervousness. Talking about her mother always made her edgy. Lyssa forced herself to smile, confident that she could hide her anxiety. It was a task she'd practiced well over the years.

"My mother never cooked a meal in her life. She was too busy working. Or sleeping." Her humor faded as she added, "Eating together wasn't something we did much of."

"Oh." He looked discomfited by the sudden change in her demeanor. "I'm sorry."

"I learned to cook from the best chefs on public television." She grinned, hoping to recoup the easy atmosphere that had been between them. "I watched a lot of TV as a kid—that happens when you don't have much parental supervision—and cooking shows were my favorite."

He grew quiet. Then he set down his spoon, his green gaze intense. Softly, he asked, "You don't like talking about your mother?"

She averted her eyes to her place setting. She straightened the butter knife that sat next to her bowl, moved her glass a fraction of an inch, playing for time as she tried to decide just how—or even if—she wanted to risk a response.

Finally, she tipped up her chin. "It's true she and I didn't have the best of relationships. But I am happy to say that we were able to work out our differences." She steeled herself. "She spent her final six months living with me."

"Oh, Lyssa," he said, reaching across the table to cover her hand with his. "I didn't mean to bring up a sad topic."

Having her childhood memories stirred was unsettling, so she remained silent. An awkwardness tumbled upon them. But she did realize, though, she found the roving of Dakota's thumb over her wrist to be very comforting.

"Isn't it amazing," he said, his words downy soft, "how all of us carry around baggage from the past?" He slid his fingers up along her forearm, his touch causing a wave of shivery heat to course across every inch of her skin.

"Take me, for instance," he continued. "I'm still trying to heal from the hurt Rose Marie inflicted on me. Never in my life had I thought I'd end up being a trophy. Wanted, not because of who I am, but for what I am."

He rambled on about himself, about his past, giving her time to recover from the melancholy she'd fallen headfirst into. It was almost as if he was apologetic about having caused this stiffness to come between them. Clearly, he didn't like it. And neither did she, so she pushed the past and all her bad feelings connected to it far away from them.

"Do you still hear from her?" she asked. "Rose Marie, I mean."

Dakota shook his head. "I don't. But I do stay in contact with friends we made together while we were married. And from what I hear, Rose Marie is still using my last name. Getting all she can from her affiliation with me—or rather, my race—even if our marriage was short-lived."

Commiseration welled up in her and she released it in a deep sigh.

"I hate lies." The words burst from him as if he had no control over them. "Deceit. Manipulations. They make me sick."

Self-consciousness invaded Lyssa like an army of stinging ants. He abhorred lies and Lyssa couldn't blame him. Yet here she was, taking advantage of his good nature, all the while keeping secrets from him. Secrets that could affect his career. That could very well affect even his safety.

She was lying to him... by omission. Refusing to alert him to what he might be up against was deceitful.

"Dakota—" she scooted to the edge of her seat and leaned toward him "—I want to thank you for all you've done for me. You've helped me to feel safe. You've shown me that I can trust you."

From the expression on his handsome face, Lyssa could tell that hearing these things from her was unexpected, yet they gave him pleasure, nonetheless. She realized that his hand was still on her forearm, his fingertips continuing to play in small semicircles over her flesh. His touch gave her courage.

"I think I've treated you unfairly by not telling you more about my ex-husband," she continued. She paused long enough to swallow, and then she squared her shoulders with resolve. "His name is Rodney Gaines. His father is Samuel Gaines. The Samuel Gaines."

A tiny pucker appeared on his forehead. "Of Gaines Industries?"

She nodded.

"Their headquarters is in California, isn't it?" He whistled, long and low. "That family is into everything. Computer technologies. Television communications. Publishing." His eyebrows shot heavenward. "That's one wealthy family."

Again, she nodded. "Money is power," she said. "Rodney has plenty of both. And he vowed to force me to return to California, to our marriage, to him, using any means available. He meant it, Dakota." Fear knifed through her, sharp as honed steel. Calmness seemed to surround Dakota like an aura. He gave her arm a reassuring squeeze.

"Okay, so your ex is a Goliath," Dakota said. "But history has shown that giants fall, Lyssa. You can't be made to go where you don't want to go, or do what you don't want to do."

His quiet strength was potent. Formidable.

He smiled. "I'm glad you told me."

Sitting here with him, she felt wrapped in a protective blanket, safe from harm. He was so easy to confide in. So easy to talk to. She was left wishing that she'd disclosed all this before now.

However, there was one secret she didn't dare reveal. She hadn't told her closest friends. She hadn't told Rodney. And she didn't plan to tell Dakota, either.

The truth was too humiliating. And if Dakota were to discover the reality of where she came from, the truth of her roots, he'd lose all respect for her. Of that she was certain.

~oOo~

Trouble arrives just when it's least expected. And anticipating turmoil today, as she basked in the October sunshine while eating her lunch on a park bench, was the last thing on Lyssa's mind. Life was good. She felt secure. Safe. Her future actually looked as if it just might be bright after all.

But the sight of the sleek yellow Aston Martin skimming along the main street of Misty Glen Reservation, an event as rare as daffodils in December, had her blood turning to ice. And seeing her ex-husband behind the steering wheel filled her to the brim with panic.

How had Rodney found her?

Miraculously, it wasn't worry over her own well-being that erupted like hot volcanic ash spewing to the forefront of her mind, but that of her friends. Rodney could put Tori Landing out of business, and Lyssa knew Tori's very survival depended upon her B&B. And Dakota! People with the kind of money Rodney had could bribe state and local officials into revoking Dakota's medical license on some phony accusation.

What might have seemed irrational thoughts to most people weren't so in Lyssa's mind. She knew who she was dealing with. Knew her fears were well-founded.

Ducking down a side street, Lyssa hurried toward the safety of the office.

She burst through the door of Dakota's office without knocking.

"He's here," she blurted, her chest rising and

falling as she gulped in air. "I've got to get my things. I've got to get out of town."

Dakota was out of his chair and at her side before she'd even finished speaking. Her mind whirled with a list of things she must do. Find her suitcase. Pack her belongings. Grab some cash from the bank. But where would she go? The destination didn't matter. She needed to be anywhere but here.

"Hold on." Dakota reached out and placed his palms firmly on her upper arms. "I'm assuming you're talking about your ex."

Her gaze was as wild as her thoughts. She was cognizant of it, but could do nothing to quell the pandemonium rampaging in her.

"Yes, yes." Her head bobbed furiously. "Rodney just drove down Main Street. I saw him. *I saw him!*"

Dakota's grip on her firmed and he forced her to look into his face.

"Stop."

The command was soft as a dove's wing, but the measure of authority it contained had her pausing.

"I want you to stop a second. Take a deep breath. Everything's going to be all right."

Just being in the same room with him helped

her mind to clear somewhat. But the trepidation flooding through every part of her threatened to drown her.

"I don't want you hurt." Hot tears welled in her eyes, fragmenting her vision. "Because of me."

Compassion tempered his intense green eyes. "What did I tell you before? You let me worry about me."

"But—"

"No buts, Lyssa," he said.

Thoughts of her ex and the threats he'd made swam in her mind, and then she thought of her child—and she was terrified!

"I have to go!" She shook herself out of Dakota's grasp, blurting, "Rodney doesn't know about the baby."

Guilt walloped her. She should have told Rodney that he was going to be a father. But if she had, she'd have never gotten away. She and her child would have been stuck in that loveless, emotionless void forever.

Silently, she pleaded for Dakota's understanding.

"The time for running is over." His expression, his tone, everything about him communicated a calm self-assurance. "We'll face him, Lyssa. Together."

Then he opened up his hand to her and waited for her reply.

There, amidst all the commotion going on in her mind and in her emotions, she felt something stir deep in her heart—something she'd never experienced before in her life.

Love.

Before this moment, she'd suspected her feelings for Dakota had intensified into something amazing. But she'd forced herself to ignore what she felt for him... how her body continued to react to him. However, in that instant, she knew she'd fallen so deeply in love with this man that there would be no turning back. Ever.

He was encouraging her to face the monsters of her past—and he was offering to face them with her.

With Dakota on her side, she felt invincible.

Silently, she slid her hand in his.

~oOo~

Together, they went looking for Rodney.

"The enemy is weaker if he's caught off guard," Dakota had declared. "The man won't expect you to search him out. He'll recover quickly, I'm sure. But going after him will be better than sitting here, waiting and worrying."

Lyssa felt comfortable putting her complete trust in Dakota's plan. They walked down the street, hand in hand. Her spine was straight and her head held high. They found Rodney leaning against the flashy car, his face tipped up to the sunshine while he took a long drag on a narrow, brown-toned cigarette.

He caught sight of Lyssa as he was exhaling a lungful of smoke.

Rodney grinned and combed his fingers through his sandy-colored hair. She remembered a time when she'd found him charming, when she'd thought he would be the answer to all her problems. But his smile had held a hard edge even then, and she wondered how she'd been blind to that. Because she'd allowed herself to be, that was how.

"Well, well, well," he said smoothly, "if it isn't my lovely wife."

His voice was like chalk and her spine was the

slate it raked against. But Dakota's fingers tightened against hers and she squared her shoulders.

"I'm not your wife anymore, Rodney," she reminded him.

As she spoke, her ex's gaze traveled to Dakota, sizing up the opposition, she guessed. Rodney snickered in a way that let everyone know he didn't feel threatened. Lyssa quickly realized that he made his first mistake by dismissing Dakota Makwa out of hand.

Rodney leisurely scanned the full length of her, his hazel eyes widening with realization when he saw the small swell of her belly.

"Seems to me that somebody in this two-bit town ought to congratulate me," he said to the few passersby who happened to be walking down the street. "I'm going to be a daddy." He looked at her. "I am the father?"

She'd meant to answer him civilly—provoking him wouldn't be a wise move—but when she opened her mouth, rebellion won out. "Unfortunately, you are."

His gaze hardened to flint. "You're coming home, Lyssa. And you're doing it now."

Her insides trembled.

"She's not going anywhere she doesn't want to go."

Lyssa knew it was impossible, but Dakota seemed to grow in bulk beside her. His voice was steely and positively unyielding.

"Look—" Rodney seemed unbothered by Dakota "—I don't know who you are, but you have no idea what you're getting mixed up in. It would be in your best interest if you just—"

"What I'm worried about" Dakota cut in, "is Lyssa's best interest. And that involves staying far away from you."

Rodney's chuckle was so cold, it was frightening. He pushed himself away from the car. "Lyssa's going to do exactly what I tell her to do. Just as she's always done. I know her better than anyone. She might leave for a while, but she always comes back." His cool gaze swiveled to hers. "Don't you, Lyssa?"

The nerves jittering in her stomach made her nauseous. She was mortified by the fact that his words held a measure of truth. Oh, he didn't know her very well at all. But she had gone back to him. She'd believed his lies. Had gotten caught up in the fantasy he'd created and she'd tried to make their marriage work a second time. That mistake had resulted in her becoming pregnant.

His gaze lit up suddenly. "I brought you a pretty."

He reached into his breast pocket. Gold and diamonds glittered in the sunlight.

"You can have it, sweetheart," he said silkily. "And all you have to do is get into the car. Now."

Humiliation had her pulling her hand from Dakota's. She lifted both hands, covered her mouth with her fingers.

Her chin trembled, and she felt bombarded with shame. She hated to admit it, but there had been a time when she'd have done exactly what he'd requested in order to have the "pretty" as he'd called the bracelet he held up as an offering.

But there's nothing pretty about a bribe, a silent voice in her head intoned. The gifts Rodney offered never failed to end up becoming double-edged swords that sliced a person into itty bitty pieces.

It had been a hard-learned lesson that had cost her a great deal.

Well, she wasn't that weak-willed, needy young

woman any longer. She had responsibilities now. She had a child to be concerned about. She may not have felt she was worth getting out of the sick relationship she and Rodney had shared, but her baby was.

"I don't want your gifts," she declared. "I don't want to have anything to do with you."

"You don't mean that." Rodney infused charisma into his tone. "We were good together, Lyssa. And you know it."

"I know no such thing."

In the blink of an eye, his whole demeanor changed yet again.

"I always intended to find you and get you back home," he said. "But finding out that we're going to have a baby, well, that just ups the ante, now doesn't it? You belong to me, Lyssa. You know you do."

Before she could respond, Dakota took a step forward.

"Lyssa doesn't belong to anyone." His hands were fisted, his shoulders tense. "Least of all you."

The image of him brought to mind a protective panther, poised and ready to strike. He was her warrior and made her feel defended. Sheltered. Loved.

It was a silly thought, she knew, and it was gone just as quickly as it had come. Like a soft, solitary breeze on an otherwise still night.

"Lyssa. Dakota."

Her head swiveled and she saw Mat coming across the street. The sheriff's arrival gave her some relief.

"Is everything okay?" Mat asked his brother.

"Just fine," Dakota answered without taking his eyes off Rodney. "Mr. Gaines is going to get into his car and he's going to drive away."

Rodney tossed his cigarette onto the street and stepped on it. "I'm not going anywhere without Lyssa and my baby."

Certain that Dakota was going to charge at Rodney, Lyssa reached out and placed a calming hand on his shoulder. He glanced at her, the concentration in his green eyes proof positive that the man had a will of iron. No wonder, Lyssa thought fleetingly, he was able to leave his first marriage when he discovered the relationship wasn't what he'd imagined it to be. He hadn't wavered as she had in her relationship with Rodney.

Silently, she begged him not to do anything foolish. She hoped he understood.

"I'm not going anywhere," she told her ex. "Now or ever. I'm staying here." She curled her fingers around Dakota's muscular biceps, purposefully bringing her plain gold wedding band into view. "With my husband."

Rodney was truly a master at disguising his emotions. Other than a small tick in his jaw, he showed no response to this revelation.

The air on that sunny afternoon drew up so tight, Lyssa wouldn't have been surprised if none of them were able to take a breath.

"The fact that you married that Indian—"

Rodney spit out the pronoun with such denigration that Lyssa felt herself flinch.

"—makes absolutely no difference to me." Now Rodney's fingers curled into his palms. "You will be returning to California. I'm not giving up on you... or my baby. Now that I know where you are, you can be sure—" his eyes narrowed ominously "—that I will be back."

He opened the door of the sports car, revved the

engine, and sped away, ejecting dust and gravel in his wake.

CHAPTER SIX

———

"I don't have anyone to blame," Lyssa told Dakota later that same evening over mugs of warm cider, "except myself."

He wasn't the kind of man to nose into someone else's business. He'd proven that by not asking questions about her past. He'd hired her. He'd taken her in. He'd *married* her. All the while suppressing the natural human instinct of wanting to know about the trouble that had her on the run. However, curiosity lit his gaze at this moment, and she could tell he was more than a little interested in the history of her failed marriage.

She sat on one end of the sofa, her feet tucked beneath her. He relaxed in an adjacent easy chair.

It had been an emotional day, trying to treat the afternoon patients while the only thing both of them wanted to do was discuss what had happened out on the street with her ex... and what they planned to do when Rodney returned as he'd promised.

Lyssa sighed. "In order for you to fully understand, I have to explain about my childhood. I had nothing, Dakota. I came from nothing. We were so poor, my mom and I. Living hand to mouth most of the time. Each week, *each day*, was a struggle to survive." It actually brought her physical heartache when she softly added, "I never knew my father."

Welling up from the furthermost chambers of her mind came the crystal-clear image of the day she'd asked about him. Her father. She'd been young. Very young. And she couldn't understand why every other child at school seemed to talk about having a daddy. Even if the parents of her classmates had split, as some parents inevitably do, her classmates talked about spending the weekend doing this or that with the man they called Dad. And Lyssa didn't have one. Had never had one.

Finally, she'd asked her mother why.

"You just don't." Her mother had shrugged, never taking her focus off her own reflection in the mirror as she applied the usual thick coat of mascara to her eyelashes.

And that was all the response Lyssa had ever received.

She hadn't bothered to ask again, and it wasn't too many years later that she'd finally worked out the full truth all on her own. And it was a truth that was too humiliating to reveal to anyone. Even to someone as wonderful as Dakota.

She sipped at the cider she now cradled between her hands.

"You can fall in love with a rich man just as well as you can a poor one." Her mouth was pursed into a thin line as she recited the advice to Dakota. "That's what my mom used to tell me. She hammered it into my head, actually."

Looking at him wasn't an option as she admitted, "I went out seeking a wealthy man. As Rodney Gaines's wife, I knew I'd never face another day of hunger. My children would want for nothing. I was sure that he could give me all the things I'd never had... could otherwise never even dream of having."

She'd decided early on that she didn't want to follow in her mother's footsteps. Lyssa was determined to find a different way, a better path on which to travel. Somehow, though, the plan she'd devised to get to that better place had become a little twisted.

She inhaled deeply, the facts of her life making her feel ill with regret. "I'm not proud of what I've done, and I'm sure not proud of the reasons why I married Rodney." She lifted her shoulder a fraction. "But it's my past. I realize that. And I'm trying to find a way to live with my actions... and the really lousy ideals I allowed to delude me for so long."

The urge to lighten the air in the room surged over her and she offered up a halfhearted grin. "I have learned from my mistakes. So that's something, at least. It would have been better for me to learn sooner rather than later. But then learning later is better than not learning at all, right?"

Her weak chuckle fell flat.

Dakota was quiet, seeming to ponder all that she'd said. Finally, he leaned forward, resting his elbows on his knees. "There's something I don't understand," he began. "You attended college. Earned your degree in nursing. You had the means to provide for yourself."

"So why continue the quest for a rich husband?" She voiced the obvious question he was leading up to.

Lyssa set her mug next to his on the coffee table. Dakota wasn't a judgmental man, but still she felt extremely self-conscious of his disapproval. She didn't dare reveal too much more, but she was determined to at least tell him enough so that he'd be able to grasp her motives.

"Abject poverty does something to a person, Dakota." She kept her tone level, her demeanor calm. She didn't want his pity, only his understanding. "My mother could barely take care of herself, let alone take care of me. I got into nursing school, yes. But scholarship money isn't easy to come by. I'd like to be able to tell you I was a genius. That organizations were clamoring to offer me a free education. But my grades were average. And I had no extracurricular activities to speak of. My college applications looked pitifully thin. In the end, I was accepted, but I had to take out loans to pay for my tuition, books, living expenses." She shook her head. "Lots of loans."

She couldn't tell what he was thinking and that left her with all sorts of worrisome vagary swirling around in her mind.

"By the time I'd graduated," she continued, "I owed tens of thousands of dollars. A mountain of debt. I started my first job. Rodney was on the board of the hospital. He was everything my mother told me to be on the lookout for. Handsome, respected, and rich. Before I knew what had happened, I was attending gala balls and charity dinners. Being dressed by honest-to-goodness clothing designers. I was rubbing elbows with senators and rock stars. I was bowled over. Completely."

Dakota was silent. Just studying her as she talked.

"Rodney's lifestyle was so far on the other end of the spectrum from where I'd grown up," she explained. "From what I was fighting my way out of." She shook her head remembering how stupefied she'd been by her ex-husband's daily existence, his days filled with boardroom meetings, his nights filled with merriment and mayhem. Her voice grated like rusty nails as she forced herself to admit, "I wanted the good life, Dakota. God help me, but I wanted it all."

He laced his fingers together. Touched the knuckle of his index finger to his chin. "So you married him." He said the words softly. "You got exactly what you wanted. The good life."

His green eyes were so keen that their hue actually seemed to deepen. The errant thought drifted through her mind that any woman who could remain unaffected by the power of his gaze—by the raw, almost animalistic power of him—must have veins filled with ice water.

He asked, "What went wrong?"

Lyssa closed her eyes as unpleasant emotions washed over her. When she raised her lids, his gaze was no less potent than it had been before.

"No sooner had we spoken our vows," she said, unable to bring her voice above a whisper, "than Rodney began acting... differently. Treating me differently."

She remembered having a hard time putting her finger on the change in him at first. The tone of his voice. The impatience in his eyes that could turn to meanness in a flash. But his behavior toward her soon made it very clear that she was no better off than her mother. No better off.

The day she'd been struck, full-force, with that realization had been a devastating one. She shoved away the horrific memory.

"He felt he owned me," Lyssa continued. "He thought he'd bought me with his millions. I was to be there for him. I wasn't to want anything for myself. No career. No friends. No identity save that of being Mrs. Rodney Gaines."

She frowned. "Once I peeled off my blinders, I saw that all the Gaines women were forced to lose themselves to their husbands. Rodney's mother bends to her husband's will purely as a means to survive. The wives of his two brothers do the same thing. And the Gaines children…"

Distress had Lyssa smoothing a protective hand over her lower abdomen as panicky tears blurred her vision. "Rodney is intimidated by his father. Scared of him, really. His brothers act the same way. And they treat their own children with the same ferociousness that they themselves receive from Samuel Gaines. They're all perpetuating some sick cycle. Like a pack of wolves constantly setting and jostling the hierarchy."

Sometime during her speech, Dakota had relaxed against the chair back. However, his eyes had never left her face for an instant.

"I put up with it for a year," she told him. "Then I left him. And while I was away from him, I brought myself up to speed so I could practice nursing. But he charmed his way back into my life. Told me he'd change. Told me things would be different. And there seemed to be no denying him." Her tone sounded far-off as she said, "It seemed so ironic that I had been the one who had gone out on the hunt. But in the end, I was the one who was trapped."

She shrugged. "There was no real love in me for Rodney. He'd destroyed the affection I'd had for him. But I'd made my bed, I decided. I would just have to lie in it. He wasn't going to stop badgering me until I surrendered. That much became clear rather quickly. However—" nerves had her swallowing jerkily "—once I discovered I was pregnant, everything changed. I don't want my child feeling afraid of his father. The idea of standing by and watching my son or daughter being raised in that kind of environment..."

The sigh she expelled came from the very depths

of her soul as a silent tear rolled down her cheek, unnoticed.

"I left Rodney for good. After doing some research, I found a judge who was both sympathetic and honest, meaning he wasn't impressed and couldn't be swayed by the Gaines fortune. In fact, Judge Burnbaum had a bit of a vendetta against my father-in-law. Years ago, Sam Gaines did all he could to keep the judge from winning his seat on the bench. Judge Burnbaum has been looking for a way to kick ol' Sam in the seat of the pants ever since." A small, sad grin crept over Lyssa's mouth. "He did that by granting me an amazingly quick divorce on the grounds of irreconcilable differences."

Lyssa sighed. "Of course, both the judge and I knew that Rodney would go ballistic over the ruling, that he'd surely contest the divorce. That's why Judge Burnbaum suggested I leave the state. He said the longer our divorce remained intact, the less chance Rodney would have of succeeding with his appeal."

After a moment of silence, she continued. "Back then, my body showed no signs of my pregnancy.

And I didn't dare tell anyone. Not even the judge. But he figured it out."

Tipping up her chin, she looked Dakota in the face. "The last thing he said to me was, '*Take care of that baby.*'"

She realized suddenly that both her hands were now splayed out over her tummy. "That's what I plan to do, Dakota. I love this baby. And I want only the best for him. Or her. I-I won't settle for anything but the best."

Her chin quivered now.

"I feel as if I'm in a deep hole," she told him, her throat growing tighter by the second. "And I know that I'm the one who's done all the digging. I put myself where I am. I'm totally to blame for my circumstances. But my child shouldn't have to suffer for my mistakes. I had to get out, Dakota."

She wanted desperately to tell him that she had no idea how to achieve what her heart desired most. In voicing the words, surely she would reveal just how weak she was at this moment, and she feared he would find her defenselessness as repugnant as she herself perceived it to be.

His forehead puckered, and she got the distinct impression that he honestly felt the pain, the regret, the fear that she was experiencing yet he didn't seem to be condemning her with a single nuance of criticism.

Finally, she breathed, "Peace. I just want to fall asleep at night unafraid of who might be chasing me. I want to be confident that my baby will be safe. I don't want to raise my child as my mother raised me. And I sure don't want to use Rodney's father's parental strategy, either. All I want is for my child to grow up in an atmosphere filled with unconditional love."

Tears slipped down her face. She couldn't say what was more crushing—the horrible facts of her past or that she'd had to reveal them to the person she most respected in the world.

He got up and came to sit on the edge of the sofa beside her.

Her voice wavered as she thinly said, "Is that too much to ask?"

There was no hesitation in him as he reached out to her. He cradled her jaw in his palm, his gaze so full of kindness that all she wanted to do was get lost in it.

"No, Lyssa. You're not asking for too much. Love. Freedom from fear. Freedom from harm.

Every mother wants those very same things for her child." His tone was assuring as he repeated, "Every mother wants them."

Something magical swirled in the heated air. Lyssa felt as if time itself froze in place. That the clock stopped ticking. All she was cognizant of was Dakota's understanding expression. Those amazing moss-green eyes seemed to hold her rapt. The feel of his skin against hers was titillating. The scent of him, heated and woodsy, wafted and spun, enveloping her, kick-starting her heart into a wild and frantic pattering. She feared he would actually hear the thumping, feel the throbbing of her pulse.

It never dawned on her to wonder how she could have been crying in despair one instant and then tumbling headlong into desire the next. All she knew was that she'd been catapulted into a hunger so strong that satiating it was her only thought.

And what had hurled her to this place of passion was the flame that had ignited in Dakota's eyes like a flash fire. Sweeping and all-consuming.

"Lyssa."

His broken tone held a myriad of emotions, and she got the sense that he was feeling baffled and troubled, joyous and determined, simultaneously.

He leaned toward her, his mouth slanting down over hers.

Heat sizzled between them, and a delicious shiver shimmered through her. His tongue skipped languidly over her lips, and she parted them in a silent invitation for him to deepen the kiss.

He tasted of the sweet tang of warm apple cider. Luscious. Spicy.

Lyssa's blood pounded, lava hot, her need growing and swelling. Running rampant. Out of control.

"I want you," he breathed against her mouth.

The words were simply too alluring to be endured.

"I've wanted you since the day we met. But—"

"No buts," she pleaded, hearing the frantic tone of her own voice. "I want you, too. I want this. No regrets, Dakota. Please."

It was as if, with those few words, she'd freed him from every trace of reserve that had been holding him back. He rose to a stand, tucked his hands beneath her body and swooped her up into his arms.

"We'll be more comfortable in my room," he said, his voice thick with desire. "In my bed."

His bedroom was cool and dark. He set her on her feet only long enough to rip the silky quilted spread from the mattress. Then he took her hand, and they sat on the edge of the bed together.

He gifted her with dozens of feather-light kisses. On her lips, her temple, her jaw, her neck. He kissed the backs of her hands, her palms, her fingertips. With each kiss, her yearning amplified until she could hear the whoosh of it in her ears, feel the heat of it throbbing through her veins. She wanted nothing less than to tear off every stitch of her clothing so he could kiss each naked inch of her.

She reached up, fumbling for the buttons of her blouse, but he stalled her efforts. Nudged her fingers away.

Frustration rose up in her sharply. However, he immediately began unfastening the buttons himself, and Lyssa's muscles relaxed. He pushed the fabric facings aside, slid the blouse from her shoulders, peeled it from her arms, tossed it to the floor.

"Your skin is like cream," he murmured, his fingertips grazing her upper arms, shoulders, the curve of her neck.

His touch was so delicious that she tilted her head, offering him the full length of her throat. He placed a searing kiss on her already hot skin. The result made her gasp with pleasure.

He traced the lacy edge of her bra first with his eyes, then with his fingertips. They were both breathless as the pads of his thumb grazed over the swell of one breast, then the other, her nipples hardening. Deftly, he freed the front hook, and the bra fell from her body. His gaze smoldered and impatience mounted inside her. She wanted to see him. Touch him.

Reaching up, she smoothed her palm over his chest, the knitted cotton soft against her skin. Then she began gathering the fabric with her fingers. With both hands, she pulled and tugged until the sweater was free and she threw it aside.

Her eyes feasted on his sinewy pectorals, his rippled abdomen, and she surrendered to the urge to touch his golden brown skin. He sucked in his breath and held it as she let her fingers meander over his chest, over his broad shoulders.

Finally, her name burst from his lips in an agonized whisper. His hand went behind her neck to support her as he urged her backward onto the mattress.

His kisses became more frantic now. The long curtain of his hair trailed about them, the silky tendrils tickling her shoulder, the sensitive skin on the inside of her elbow. She reached up and combed her fingers through the sleek, luxurious locks, fanning them outward, felt them dance and skitter across her skin.

Heated current zipped through her body, her muscles strained up toward his touch, toward his kiss. She wanted more. And she wanted it now. The frustration and longing raging in her must have been evident in her frenzied gaze.

"Wait," he urged softly. "Wait."

With slow, deliberate fingers, he unfastened her jeans. He tucked his thumbs oh-so-intimately into the stretchy waistband and tugged the pants free of her body. And although all she wore now were her silky panties, she still felt hindered by too much fabric. Looking down the length of herself, she suffered a moment of self-consciousness. Could he find the swell of her pregnant body desirable?

But the feeling was fleeting because the fact that

he found her—all of her—pleasing was blatantly expressed in his eyes.

"You... now," she implored in a rush, unable to quell the urgency she endured. "It's your turn."

He gifted her with the sexiest of grins. "Yes, so it is my turn."

In order to take off his trousers, he had to get up. He stood there by the bed a moment, merely gazing at her, his ravenous eyes traveling down the full length of her. Lyssa felt his wanting stare almost as if it were a physical touch.

After he removed the last vestiges of his clothing, she witnessed the indisputable proof of his need of her. He eased himself down beside her. The atmosphere of the room crackled with the electric passion pulsing around them, through them, between them. Their desire was a connection. A bond. A union that drew them closer and closer.

She couldn't even smile now as she murmured, "I think it's my turn again."

"Oh, yes."

He sounded winded, as if he'd run a long distance. And Lyssa liked thinking that she affected him in this manner.

"Yes," he told her, "it's your turn. Unless, of course—" he grinned wickedly now "—you'd rather I did the honors."

She just shook her head.

He eased back a bit, resting his upper body on one elbow, his mossy eyes glittering with expectation.

Slipping her index fingers beneath the peach-colored lace, she slid her panties slowly, erotically, down the length of her lower body, over hips, thighs, knees, calves. Her throaty chuckle echoed off the walls as she caught the tiny strip of fabric on the bridge of one foot and flung it with a quick and tiny kick.

Their eyes met. And held.

As if he couldn't keep his hands off her any longer, he rolled toward her. The heat of him, the weight of him made her delirious with joy. The ache that had been, until now, dull and low in her belly, flared like a dangerous bonfire needing, no, demanding to be quenched.

"I need you," he said.

And Lyssa gasped with relief. "That's good," she whispered between kisses. "Because I feel the same."

She let herself get lost in his kiss, lost in his touch, knowing this would be one long and scrumptious night.

~oOo~

Lyssa woke the next morning in a tangle of sheets, the cotton soft against her naked skin. Memories flooded her brain, sensual images flashed, soft caresses and moans, breathless sighs, strokes and touches that left her weak. A languid smile tugged at the corners of her mouth. Yes, last night would be unforgettable, indeed!

She looked over toward Dakota's side of the bed, the mere sight of his broad, muscular back rekindling the embers of her desire. But she decided it was too early to wake him. He had patients to treat today. He needed his rest. Especially since he'd performed so well—and so long—last night. Lyssa couldn't stifle her grin.

Lyssa started when his cell rang. Dakota groped for and picked up the phone, identifying himself. After listening for only a moment, he sat up on the edge of the mattress.

She rose up on one elbow. "What is it, Dakota?"

His back was still to her and he tensed at the sound of her voice. Whatever the matter was, it must be serious as he didn't respond to her query.

"How long has she been in the E.R.?" he asked of whomever it was on the other end of the phone line.

Dakota leaned over as he talked and snatched up the clothing he'd discarded so carelessly last night.

"Okay, who's with her?" he asked. "No, I mean which doctor?" He clutched the waistband of his pants in his free hand and struggled into them. "Good. She knows what she's doing. Do you know how many of the berries Grace ate?" Another slight pause. "Okay, just sit tight and I'll be right there."

Lyssa realized suddenly that Dakota hadn't turned to face her once. Hadn't acknowledged her presence. He hadn't even looked at her. A strange reserve came over her and she pulled the sheet up high to cover herself.

He tucked the phone into his pocket and headed for the door.

"Hey," she called out to him. "What's going on?"

"Mat's daughter," he said, but he'd already disappeared down the hallway.

"Your niece ate some berries? What kind of berries?" She sat up, pinning the sheet to her tightly. She called out, "Is she okay?"

"Don't know."

Water ran in the bathroom sink, and she heard the sounds of him scrubbing his teeth.

"Seems yesterday in school," he called, "Grace learned how the Kolheeks used to live off the land, foraging for their food. She got up this morning and decided she'd do the same. Mat found her with red berry juice all over her clothes. She was standing in a bunch of poke weed."

"That's poisonous," she breathed even though she knew he'd never hear her comment. Concern chilled her body and goose bumps erupted on her skin.

He bustled back into the room, opening the closet and jerked a clean shirt from its hanger. She watched him stuff his arms into the sleeves, straighten the collar, fasten the buttons.

Still he didn't look in her direction. Anxiety for the little girl mingled inside her along with a niggling doubt about last night. Why couldn't he bring himself to look at her?

Did he regret making love to her?

Embarrassment flooded her from the soles of her feet to the roots of her hair. She felt hot, prickly with the sudden outbreak of perspiration.

"I've got to go," he told her, grabbing up socks and shoes.

Of course, he was alarmed for his niece. So was Lyssa. But didn't she deserve one second of his time? After what they had shared last night, wasn't she worth a quick glance? Just one soft word?

Sudden angst had her stomach tensing. "D-do you want me to come along with you?"

"Don't have time to wait," he said over his shoulder. "Besides, I need you to take care of things at the office until I can get back. I'll call you as soon as I know something."

And with that, he was gone.

Lyssa looked around the room, felt the booming silence almost mocking her. She was very conscious of her nakedness and keenly aware of how unrestrained she'd behaved during those long night hours. She shouldn't have made love with Dakota. Not after revealing to him how she'd gone out hunting for a rich husband who could keep her in material things.

A groan rose up in her throat as humiliating

tears blurred her vision. Surely he thought she was a tramp who was willing to sleep with any man who came down the pike. Any man who was good enough to provide what she needed.

Her stomach knotted.

No matter how hard she tried, it seemed she was destined to end up just like her mother.

CHAPTER SEVEN

Dakota had never been more disappointed in himself. Last night, he'd lost control. Completely.

He parked the car, let himself into the house and went directly to the bathroom, stripped and stepped into the shower. The hot needles of water felt good as the spray sluiced over his body. And as he lathered himself with soap, memories of making love to Lyssa bombarded him.

She was a passionate and giving lover who offered herself with abandon. The soft and uninhibited moans that had issued from deep in her throat... the way she'd arched her back, striving to reach that place where they had both tumbled over from the precipice into the deep and steamy void of desire. She'd stirred his blood in such a primal fashion that it had been hard for him to take his time. To take it slow. To savor every luscious second.

Even now, his body quickened.

Could it be, a small voice echoed from the back of his brain, that Lyssa is the woman meant just for you? Could there be something to the legend called Woman of the Heart?

Swallowing a curse, he shoved the ridiculous notion aside. There was no such thing. The story was just that. A story. And a dangerous one, at that. Hadn't he learned the hard way that love only ripped the heart to shreds? Love left a man wounded and bleeding. He didn't need that.

With a new firmness of thought, he put his mind to getting himself dried, shaved, and dressed. Dwelling on his mistakes would do no good. He'd have to apologize to Lyssa for his lack of control. Try to explain this mess that he'd made of their arrangement. And he'd have to do his damnedest not to let it happen again. But doing so would be difficult. Lyssa was a beautiful woman. A desirable woman who made his soul sing.

Dakota shook his head with disgust. He'd better

get to work before those fanciful thoughts invaded his mind once again.

He went into the building by the back entrance, not seeing Lyssa, his receptionist, or any patients. He was actually relieved to have a few moments alone to calm his mind before having to focus his attention on illnesses, complaints, symptoms, and prescriptions.

The sight of Lyssa standing in front of his desk stopped him in his tracks.

"How's your niece?" she asked.

"Grace's going to be just fine," he told her. "She pitched a fit over having the contents of her stomach pumped—" Dakota lifted one shoulder slightly "—but the procedure was necessary."

Seconds ticked by and the air between them stiffened with acute awkwardness. Something needed to be said. The events of last night needed to be mentioned. But for the life of him, Dakota simply couldn't find the right words. Regret gathered in his chest like a cement block, and before he could stop himself, his gaze dropped to the tiled floor like a heavy stone.

It was her sigh that made him look her in the face. The sound of it held such woe. He guessed she was feeling as remorseful about what had happened between them as he. He hated thinking he'd led her to participate in something she now despaired over.

However, when she spoke she was as professional as ever.

"We were able to shuffle around some appointments," she told him briskly. "But Mr. Mason and little Danny Brunner really needed to see you, so I've got them waiting. I hope that's okay."

"That's fine," he assured her.

Silence swirled around them, thick as wood smoke and just as choking.

Her spine straightened. "I want you to know," she told him, her gaze sliding from his, but only a fraction of a second later her chin tipping up and her golden eyes leveling on him once again, "no matter what it might look like, I do not make a habit of sleeping with every man who comes into my life. I assure you of that."

There was so much emotion in her words. Shame mingled with determination. Humiliation merged with an underlying hint of confidence. Her body language told him that although she regretted her behavior last night, she was proud of who she was, of what she believed in.

I'm moral. I'm honest.

Those were the unspoken points she seemed set on making.

"I never—"

"I was simply responding," she interrupted boldly, "to the attraction that's been tugging at us since I first came to work for you. You've felt it. I know you have. You can't deny it."

So surprised was he by what she said that the words he'd been about to utter died in his throat.

"I won't let you deny it. Because, if you do, that will turn me into something I'm not."

Tears glistened in her brown eyes, and Dakota finally realized that she was feeling terribly culpable for what had happened between them. And she was almost frantic for him to accept some of the blame.

He was happy to do just that. In fact, he'd intended on taking all the blame, but before he could, she smoothed agitated fingers over her hair, tucking a wayward strand behind her ear. She paced two steps away from him, then turned back to face him.

"I mean," she continued, "I know we went into this as a purely platonic deal. A business agreement. I'd scratch your back and you'd scratch mine."

As soon as the words came out of her mouth, her lips parted. Her milky complexion became inflamed with embarrassment.

In a rush, she persisted, "This marriage was meant as nothing more than mere convenience for both of us. I'd help you get those women off your back. And you'd help me out with... my problems."

She swallowed, and as he watched the hollow of her throat seize and relax, he was reminded of the honeyed taste of her flesh when he'd kissed the length of her neck.

"I know you said that you were through with relationships." She moistened her lips, a nervous crease drawing her eyebrows together. "But, Dakota—" her tone lowered, her lovely eyes widened "—I've got to tell you, I-I've begun to feel... something. Something shadowy. Mysterious. Something meaningful."

Again she swallowed, frowning with her inability, or was that reluctance, to express herself.

Her voice softened as she added, "I think you have, too. Haven't you?"

The tone of her tiny question was tinged with beseeching, and Dakota recognized that she was desperate for him not to oppose her. That, for some reason, her dignity hinged on his answer. However, he was too stunned—no, *aghast* would better describe his reaction to the suggestion she was making.

Just moments before seeing her, he'd decided that their lovemaking had been a total mistake. A blunder that couldn't be repeated... no matter how pleasurable the experience had been.

"No," he answered firmly, shaking his head. "No, Lyssa. That's not what's happening here."

He'd intended to continue, but his refusal to agree with her about the mysterious something they were supposed to be feeling for each other sent her fingers flying to cover her mouth. Her eyes grew haunted, her chin trembled, and she fought back tears, all evidence of her mortification. Clearly, she regretted having revealed herself to him. She attempted to dart around him. To escape further embarrassment, he surmised, or to avoid having to look in his face any longer, or disclosing any more of her feelings.

"Hold on," he said. The warm, luscious scent of her made his insides tighten, and he silently cursed the magnitude of his physical need of her. But that was all it was. A physical urge. A craving that could be controlled—that would be controlled.

"We've got patients waiting. We can talk about this later."

But he secured her forearm in his grasp and spun her around to face him.

"We'll talk about this now." He hoped his calm tone camouflaged the riot of emotion warring in his belly.

He wanted to pull her to him. Kiss her senseless. Make her moan and writhe in his arms as she had last night. But that was impossible. She thought there was a possibility of a real and lasting relationship between them. Succumbing to his desire for her would only fuel this fairytale she'd conjured.

He had to nip this in the bud. Right this second.

"First of all," he told her, zeroing in on her face to make his point very clear, "I do not hold you responsible for what happened between us last night. You were upset. Distraught."

Disgust at his behavior had him combing agitated fingers through his hair. "I was supposed to be helping you. Protecting you. Instead, I... I—" He didn't want to reveal just how overwhelming his passion for her had been, fearing he'd encourage her notion that there was something between them. "I took advantage of the situation. I took advantage of you. And for that, I'm terribly sorry."

He'd expected his explanation to ease her embarrassment. She wasn't to blame. *He* was. Totally. However, she only looked more stricken. Sometime during his short monologue, he couldn't say when exactly, she'd pulled her arm from his grasp.

Guilt walloped him. "Look, Lyssa," he continued, "I tried to explain to you how I feel about relationships."

Her shoulders squared and her chin tipped up. "Yes. You're distrustful of women. Because of your ex-wife."

She'd summed it up into a nice, neat little

package, and the manner in which she spoke told him that she felt his motivation was flimsy.

"It's more than just Rose Marie," he felt compelled to say.

Lyssa provided, "Your mother."

He was taken aback and knew his expression clearly displayed it.

"You mentioned your mother once," she added. "Told me she'd betrayed you. Back when you first told me about Rose Marie."

"I did?" He hadn't remembered doing so. But he must have mentioned his mother. Otherwise, how would she know? It amazed him Lyssa remembered. "Yes, well... Norma Makwa was a deceitful woman. Not just to me. But also to the man I called father."

"I don't understand. The man you called father..."

It was obvious that the awkwardness she'd felt just a moment before was replaced now by acute curiosity.

Dakota sighed. So few people knew his story. He'd discussed his suspicions with his brother, Mat. But he hadn't gone to his grandfather. He hadn't wanted Grayson to look down on him. To treat him any differently than anyone else. And pointing out his "disparity" just might make that come to fruition.

"I've always known I was different," he began slowly. "For as long as I can remember. I was teased about my green eyes. Eyes so different from those of my full-blooded Kolheek relatives."

He paused, giving her the chance to take in all the implications of his story. And when she continued to look a bit confused, he decided to delve further into the murkiness of his past.

"When I was young, I asked my mother how I came to have green eyes. And she waved off my concern. Told me that there must be European genes somewhere in the Makwa family tree and that's where I'd inherited my eye color from."

Anger rolled over him, just as it did every time he thought about his mother's lies.

He moistened his lips before going further. "After my parents died, I went to live with Grayson. My grandfather filled my life with the rich tapestry that was our ancestry. A history of brave men and women who fought to survive against all odds." He felt his jaw tighten. "Nowhere was there any mention of European ancestors."

He couldn't tell what Lyssa was thinking, but he was too wrapped up in his misery to stop now.

"The fact that I'm different," he said, "that I never quite looked like everyone else around me continued to niggle at me. I learned all about dominant and recessive genes in med school. There's no conclusion to come to, Lyssa, other than that my mother was unfaithful to Will Makwa... the man who raised me until he died, the man who allowed me to call him father even though his blood doesn't run through my veins."

His gaze narrowed. "My mother was deceitful. She was a liar. And I live with the proof of her conniving ways each and every time I look in the mirror."

Lyssa was silent a moment, evidently taking in all of the awful truth he was disclosing. Finally, she crossed her arms over her chest and looked him directly in the eye.

"I'm sorry you've been hurt, Dakota," she told him. "I'm sorry you've been used. And I'm sorry you've been lied to. But my name isn't Rose Marie. And it isn't Norma, either." Her honey-brown gaze set and her chin lifted a fraction. "And if you refuse to accept the plain and obvious facts, the truth that's staring you cold in the face, then I feel sorry for you for that, too."

With determined steps, she moved to his office door, opened it, exited the room, and closed the door firmly behind her, leaving him all alone in the sudden and bizarre silence.

~oOo~

Keep busy. Just keep your mind occupied.

During the past several days, Lyssa had done her best to do just that. If her hands and her thoughts were engaged, then she wouldn't dwell on the terrible and humiliating facts.

She paged through the listings on the website without even seeing the big bold advertisements. A groan welled up within her and she did her best to suppress it. She didn't want anyone, least of all Dakota, to know just how miserable she was feeling.

Had she really revealed her heart to him so openly? Yes, she had, came the dismal answer, and she'd done so only to have him reject her, point-blank.

Resting her elbow on the kitchen table, she sank

her forehead onto her fingertips and did what she could to rub away the anxiety and regret. Tension had built up in her to such a degree that her head ached.

Oh, if only she and Dakota had met earlier in her life. Maybe she could have avoided Rodney and the whole Gaines family altogether. Maybe, just maybe, she could have evaded the mess she'd made of her life if only—

"What are you doing?"

Lyssa started, but quickly recovered herself. As Dakota entered the kitchen, a swirl of energy seemed to follow on his heels.

An unmistakable awkwardness. That ever-present awareness.

He'd made it plain that he was willing to endure the awkwardness between them. To act as if it didn't bother him in the least. But the awareness? Sometimes Lyssa felt as if she was being plucked at by physical fingers, physical vibrations that hummed and pulsated. There was no way she or Dakota could keep from noticing it.

Well, if he was determined to ignore this overwhelming sensitivity, this potent attraction, then she could, too, damn it. She could, too!

"I'm searching the internet for an obstetrician." She pressed the page down button on the laptop, realizing that she'd lost focus on her chore long ago. "However, it looks like I'm going to have to drive all the way to—"

"You don't have to drive anywhere," he told her quietly. "I'll be happy to act as your doctor."

Lyssa forced her eyes back to the screen. She didn't want to feel all soft and mushy inside. She wanted to be irritated with him. With his refusal to see what they might have together if they allowed their relationship to develop, if they gave themselves the chance to explore...

He has good reason to avoid doing that, a quiet voice in her head silently reminded her.

Maybe he did. But understanding his motive didn't make the situation any easier.

"Do you think that would be wise?" she asked without looking at him.

"Anything else would be silly." He sat down at the table, reached over, and covered her forearm with his warm fingers. "Why spend the money? And why go to the trouble of traveling three towns over? I'm perfectly capable of managing your health care while you're pregnant. And I've delivered lots of babies."

"But, Dakota—"

"I insist."

She sensed the warm mass of him move closer to her. He touched her chin, forced her eyes to meet his, and she thought she'd never experienced such compassion as she saw in his expression.

"Lyssa, this will be a doctor-patient relationship," he assured her. "Period."

She heard his proclamation, but she wasn't sure she believed it. Oh, he believed the statement. Every lousy word was chiseled in the set of his jaw. However, he was refusing to acknowledge just how compelling this allure was that was tugging at them.

"Come on." His tone was light, urging, as he scooped up her hand in his. "The office is closed. We could—"

Dark qualms skulked about in the recesses of her mind, forcing her to hesitate, to avert her eyes from his.

But he was determined. "I've heard that nurses make terrible patients," he chuckled softly, "but this is ridiculous." He tugged her from the chair.

Reluctance made her feet feel leaden, but she followed him down the hall that led to the medical offices.

Lyssa was impressed by his professional demeanor as he noted all her pertinent information. He scolded her for not having seen a doctor before the end of her first trimester. However, he seemed to understand when she explained that she'd been too busy running away from her ex and he was appeased when she assured him that she'd been taking her vitamins religiously. He took her blood pressure, managing the cuff and gauge of the sphygmomanometer expertly. And he didn't even laugh at her when she insisted on removing her shoes before being weighed. She thought that maybe, just maybe, the two of them could get through this patient-physician relationship without desire encroaching on them.

"I should listen to your heart," he said.

The moment his fingers brushed her skin, Lyssa felt her pulse skitter. Memories of the night they had made love came flooding into her brain. Self-consciousness had her staring off into a far corner of the room as extremely carnal images refused to be banished.

However, the fact that she wasn't looking at him only heightened her tactile sense. She became even more aware of the heat of his fingers. The silk of his skin against hers. The warm male scent of him. The tickle of his exhalation against her jaw. And she went utterly still when she realized... he was trembling.

Boldly, she tipped up her chin and leveled her gaze on his. But his moss-green eyes slid from hers.

The air was thick with sensation. Hazy with it. But Lyssa would rather have died than to be the first to admit it. She'd made that mistake once. She certainly wouldn't be facing that kind of humiliation again anytime soon.

"Sounds good," he murmured. "Nice strong rhythm. Now, let's listen to the baby."

Alarm had Lyssa panicky, but she eased herself back onto the exam table and automatically began loosening her clothing. She pulled up her blouse to just beneath her breasts and tugged her trousers down onto her hips. Shyness oozed to the surface, and she did what she could to swallow back her nervousness. She looked up at him through half-closed lashes, and she was shocked to find Dakota staring at her abdomen.

At four months pregnant, she certainly wasn't huge, but her tummy did have a distinctive swell. She remembered the different times he'd touched her. Placing a protective hand on her belly once while reassuring her. Smoothing velvet fingers over her tiny bulge when they'd made love.

She felt timid, and the allure spinning and dancing in the exam room only heightened the anxiety in her. What was he thinking? Why had he grown so utterly still? Was he, too, remembering the times he'd touched her?

Unable to stand the silence any longer, she spoke his name.

He blinked, and she got the impression that time slowed to a crawl. His gaze roved over her navel, up her torso, over her breasts, her throat, her chin, hovered at her lips and then latched onto her eyes. His expression was fraught with profound emotion. However, when his silence continued, Lyssa knew he was determined to keep whatever he was feeling to himself.

The muscle in the back of his jaw clenched. He was a strong man, she'd learned that much while working with him... in being married to him. If he chose to fight the desire throbbing in the atmosphere, she was certain he'd conquer it.

He swallowed, and his nostrils flared when he took a deep inhalation. Only after he'd evidently tamed the emotions warring in him did he touch her.

His palms were warm against her stomach, his fingers gentle as he probed and pressed against her tummy. His gaze and his focus was on the exam now, the beguiling magnetism having retreated into the corners of the room where it lingered, waiting.

The ultrasound stethoscope chilled her skin as he slid it from one side of her stomach to the other, searching. Finally, a fuzzy-sounding rhythm filled the room and Lyssa gasped.

There was something about hearing her child's heartbeat for the first time that made her own heart ache. Her eyes welled with happy tears.

"That's my baby," she exclaimed.

"It is." Dakota's sexy mouth pulled with a grin. "It's a wonderful sound."

"Oh." Why was she crying? "It is. It really is." Joy curled inside her, filling her with warmth. Without thought, she pressed her hand to her tummy. "I love this baby," she said, the words tripping from her tongue without thought. "And I'm never going to let anyone hurt him. Ever."

She was speaking of Rodney and his family. She knew that Dakota understood what she meant. There was no need to explain.

Maternal instinct crowded out all other emotion, and Lyssa lay on the exam table with her eyes closed reveling in dreams of what kind of life she wanted for her child. Her sigh was contented, and when she lifted her eyelids, she saw that Dakota was watching her.

"So," she said, smiling, "do I pass the test? Is my baby healthy?"

"I give you both my stamp of approval."

He turned his back to her then, focusing on making notes in her electronic file and giving her time to get her clothing arranged.

She was sitting up on the table now, buttoning up her blouse. Sheer happiness had her heart feeling light. All she wanted was for everyone in the whole world to experience this kind of soul-deep elation, and it was with this motivation only that she decided to broach what she knew would be a sticky subject.

"Dakota," she began.

"Yes." He didn't turn to face her, just continued to type.

"I've been thinking about something. Something you said."

As soon as his green eyes were on her, caution reared its head like a frightening snake. But Lyssa refused to back down. Dakota deserved to be happy. He needed to hear this.

"Those things you told me," she continued, "about your mother." Leeriness narrowed his eyes a bit, but she barreled forward. "I know that you've spent a lot of time feeling angry and betrayed. But I want you to know that, well, that what you are doing isn't very healthy. You're hurting yourself by holding on to all these negative feelings."

He looked dubious.

"I know," she told him. "I've had to forgive my own mother's transgressions. And it's because of that that I'm able to give you this advice."

She could see that he still wasn't convinced.

"You need to talk to someone." Absently, she tugged at the hem of her blouse. "You need to find out the truth. Go to Mat. Or better yet, your grandfather. Grayson might be able to tell you exactly what happened. He just might solve the mystery you've been living with, to tell you how you came to have green eyes."

Ire simmered to the surface of his expression.

"I want you to be happy, Dakota," she said, sincerity in her tone. "That's what I want for you."

For the longest time, he was silent. When he finally spoke, his voice grated. "I appreciate your concern. Honestly, I do. But—" he shook his head, his long silky hair swaying gently "—I don't know, Lyssa. I just don't know if I can do what you're asking."

CHAPTER EIGHT

———

Dakota heaved on the crowbar with all his might and felt a small sense of satisfaction at the sound of wood cracking, a rusty nail popping from its confines. He'd come out into the backyard looking for something to destroy. The old gazebo, built years before he'd bought the house, had been constructed of inferior lumber. Rot ate at the foundation in places, creeping vines hid most of the latticework. He'd never used the structure and had always intended on tearing it down but had never gotten around to doing so.

A sledgehammer and crowbar were perfect tools to help him vent some of his pent-up agitation. The tension was getting to him. Oh, Great One in heaven, help him, but it was becoming more than he could take.

Over the past week, the sexual frustration alone had been enough to have his skin crawling with need. He watched Lyssa at the office by day, hungered for her at night. He lay in his bed, his body throbbing. He yearned for what he couldn't have, knowing he was separated from her by the mere thickness of a bedroom wall. He tossed for hours before sleep would overtake him. And even then his torment didn't end. His dreams were filled with sharp and explicit images: the sight of her naked flesh, the sound of her desirous moans, the smell of her silky hair, the taste of her luscious mouth.

With a groan of his own, Dakota tossed aside the crowbar, picked up the sledgehammer, and swung it with all his might. Wood splintered, slivers flying.

Why couldn't he control this desire? It was like a rain-swollen river that refused to be contained, rising up over its banks and flooding all of the surrounding countryside. That's exactly what it felt like, because there wasn't an area of Dakota's life that wasn't affected by his attraction to this woman.

He didn't want to want her. Yet, if he were to be completely honest, he'd have to admit that there was more to all of this than mere physical attraction.

He'd learned so much about her. Life had dealt her some hard knocks. She'd made some wrong choices. But she was trying to get her life straightened out.

Everyone deserved a second chance.

He wasn't too worried about her past giving her too much problem. He'd met her ex. Rodney Gaines might have more money than the devil himself, but wealth could only go so far. Dakota was of the opinion that Gaines was a weak-willed man, a pathetic bully who probably wouldn't show his face at Misty Glen rez again.

Still, Lyssa worried about what her ex-husband might do now that he knew she was pregnant. And Lyssa's worries were Dakota's worries. He was honor-bound to protect her. And he planned to do just that.

She was sweet and loving. Giving and kind. She deserved his support.

He took another frustrated swipe at the gazebo. If anyone were to be privy to his thoughts, he just might be accused of being smitten with his pretty young wife.

"No!" He growled the word out loud.

Love hurt. And he would not allow himself to be vulnerable to that kind of pain again. Ever.

"Hello, my son."

Dakota turned, saw his grandfather and felt his scowl soften. "Hello, Grandfather."

Grayson Makwa's arrival didn't startle Dakota in the least. All his life, this is what he'd experienced. During his times of great mental turmoil, if he did not seek out his grandfather, Grayson would end up just showing up, seemingly right out of the blue. It became obvious to Dakota very early on that his grandfather had the gift of sight when it came to his grandchildren. Just how clear his "visions" were, Dakota couldn't say. But the shaman's gift was there, nonetheless.

"I've been expecting you," the old man said. "I feel as if it is your time to seek. And learn. And grow. But I fear you're being stubborn."

A small, faint chuckle of irony erupted from Dakota's throat. He put down the heavy hammer and sighed. "Yes. I guess you could say that. But it was only because I didn't know how to ask you about what has been bothering me."

Grayson's chocolate-brown eyes glistened with affection. "The journey begins," he said softly, "with but a single step."

In that instant, Dakota realized two things: Lyssa had been right, he needed to talk about this, to finally discover the truth; and his grandfather was right, as well. The truth would never be found in his continued silence.

Turning to face his grandfather fully, Dakota said, "I'm different."

"We are all different, my son. Yet, we are all the same."

But the sadness that filled Grayson's eyes reflected an unmistakably profound knowledge. Clearly, the old man sensed where the conversation would eventually lead.

"I'm different from all my Kolheek brothers and sisters," Dakota pressed.

Sorrow seemed to round Grayson's shoulders. "Yes, my son. Yes, you are."

Dakota felt the need to brace himself. He was about to learn the full extent of his mother's betrayal. "Your mother never wanted you to know."

Anger simmered inside Dakota. "I'll bet she didn't."

Grayson seemed puzzled by his grandson's ire. Then he surmised, "Sometimes the truth can do more harm than good, Dakota. But it seems to me you need to know what happened. In fact, it could very well be that the truth has been too long in coming."

That's exactly how Dakota felt. He nodded slowly, silently.

"Let us walk." Grayson lifted his hand and gestured toward the forest. Dakota didn't hesitate to follow.

On the rez, thick thatches of woodland were never far off. The Kolheek believed that trees and bushes, wildlife and running water, gave much more than merely fresh air and sustenance. Nature offered wisdom; if one was willing to truly listen.

"Your brother was just over a year old when you were conceived," the old man began. "Norma Makwa had been a dedicated wife and mother. Never leaving her husband or Mat once in all those months after giving birth to her first son. Some of her friends planned a weekend shopping trip to Boston and they invited your mother along. She'd led a pretty sheltered life. Had always been frightened of the city, you see, feeling much more at home here in the mountains, among her own people. But what young woman can resist the promise of a little fun and excitement?"

Dakota's jaw clenched. So it was as he feared. His mother had submitted to the lure of pleasure.

The very tone of Grayson's voice seemed to grow heavy. "The women returned early. And your mother was forever changed."

Dakota remained silent.

"She was taken," his grandfather's voice was whisper soft, as though he couldn't bear to speak the words, "against her will."

The world began a wild spin. Dakota stopped, whirled a quarter turn and clamped his hand on his grandfather's arm. Whether or not he meant to halt Grayson's forward movement, or support himself, Dakota couldn't say for sure.

"She was raped?"

The older man's only answer was to close his eyes and swallow with obvious difficulty, emotion vibrating from him.

Finally, Grayson was able to continue. "She refused to go to the Boston police. Insisted, instead, that her friends bring her home. She was silent for weeks. I counseled her every day. Prayed for her. *With* her. I tried to get her to open up to me. To talk about what had happened to her.

"She was so afraid that your father was going to leave her. Afraid that the entire tribe would look down on her, as if she were dirty. She felt... soiled."

Riotous feelings bashed and clattered inside him, but Dakota could find no words that seemed right for the moment.

"Norma had always been a fragile creature," the old man said, "but after her trip to Boston... after that harrowing experience, she became as delicate as bone china. Your father—" Grayson's gaze glittered with pride "—I was so proud of my son. He said all the right things. His love for your mother was strong. He made her understand that the body is just a shell... like armor, is what he called it. Someone dented and scratched her armor, your father told her. But that didn't make her a different person. She was still the same inside. Untouched. And whole."

Dakota felt overwhelmed. It was all too much to take in.

"Why didn't anyone ever tell me?"

Love lit his grandfather's dark eyes. "She didn't want you to know, Dakota. She never wanted you to know. She was adamant that you would never face the stigma of being the product of rape. She wanted more than anything else for you to have a normal childhood."

In his mind's eye, Dakota remembered how he'd responded to Lyssa's desires for her child. Love, freedom from fear, freedom from harm, those were the things that every mother wanted for her child.

Even his own.

Grayson continued, "It was the pregnancy that brought her out of her depression. You saved your mother, Dakota. She looked on you as a gift from The Great Spirit. She believed that everything happens for a reason. I believe that, too. You needed to be born. You needed a womb in which to grow. A mother to love you. She was chosen. She was grateful to have been chosen."

In a haze, Dakota eased himself down on a fallen log. Grayson sat down beside him.

"Your mother loved you." The old man placed

a reassuring hand on his grandson's knee. "Your father loved you, too. My son raised you as his own, and there was never a doubt that he'd do anything other than that."

"I-I've been angry with her." Dakota's voice was dry and rusty. "I thought she betrayed—"

"I realize that now," Grayson interrupted. "I should have told you the truth long ago."

Dakota knew the powerful anguish he was feeling was reflected in his eyes, in the stiffness of his whole body.

"The important thing you must remember, my son, is that you were loved. The circumstances surrounding your creation have nothing whatsoever to do with who you are. You are a good person. An intelligent man who has helped many people. And you will help many more over your lifetime. You have a good heart. Skilled hands. An intelligent mind. Those are the things you must contemplate."

Dakota understood what his grandfather attempted to convey. But he wasn't as upset about being the result of rape as he was disturbed by how he'd totally misjudged his mother.

"I've thought terrible things about her," he told Grayson. "For years I've been resentful."

Grayson patted Dakota's shoulder. "You can make it right, Dakota. You know what to do."

~oOo~

In a flash, Lyssa was awake, alert. She lay in the darkness, still and barely breathing, wondering what it was that had nudged her into consciousness. Low, melodious tones seeped into her brain and had her sitting up on the edge of the mattress. Without thought, she scooted her feet into her slippers, snatched up her robe, and was out the bedroom door even as she slipped her arms into the sleeves and tied the sash.

The house was dark and quiet, and Lyssa continued to search for the faint but haunting tune.

The orange glow coming from outside drew her to the window. Flames licked at the night sky. A small fire burned at the far end of the backyard. And it was from there that the poignant strains were emanating.

A shiver coursed over every inch of her skin

when she realized that it was Dakota's voice she heard. He was out there in the night... singing.

She hadn't seen him all day long. Earlier in the afternoon, he'd been tearing down the old gazebo. She'd watched as he'd disappeared into the thicket of trees with his grandfather. But he hadn't come in for dinner, and he still hadn't made an appearance when she'd decided to go to bed.

She opened the back door and the hinges squeaked like tiny mice. Light from inside the house arrowed into the darkness. Dakota's singing ceased.

He sat cross-legged facing the flames. He swiveled his head to look her way, his long hair glistening, the fire turning his bare upper body a tawny copper.

Dakota motioned for her to join him, and Lyssa didn't hesitate.

"I'm sorry I woke you," he said.

"Don't be. I'm sorry I disturbed you." She got the feeling that something about him was... different. The tension in him had eased. "You disappeared today with Grayson. I've been thinking about you."

"I needed some time alone." His gaze drifted to

the fire, then he looked back up at her. He patted the ground beside him, inviting her to sit.

The grass was cool and she huddled into her robe. "It's chilly out here, but the fire is toasty."

"Yes," he agreed.

There it was again, she thought, recognizing that familiar awareness that constantly purred between them.

Finally, he said, "You'll be happy to know that I spoke with my grandfather about my mother."

Was that the cause of this lightness she sensed about him? She certainly hoped so.

"I've wronged her," he said, his tone heavy with regret. "Terribly."

Silence stretched out, and Lyssa didn't know what to say. She wanted to ask him why he'd built the fire. Why and what he chanted. Why he sat out here in the darkness. But all of those inquiries seemed too personal to voice.

Nearly another full minute passed before she was able to say, "Your song... it was beautiful. You were singing in your native language?"

He nodded. "I don't know much Algonquian. But Grandfather taught me some. That was the Prayer of Reparation. I am making amends to my mother's spirit. The smoke from the fire carries my sorrowful words to her. Hopefully, she will forgive me."

The concept was touching, and Lyssa smiled. "I should leave you in peace." But when she moved to get up, he reached out and touched her forearm.

"I'd like you to stay," he said. "It is only because of you that I'm able to put this to rest. To let go of my anger and all the bitterness. It's because of you that I realized my offense, that I'm able to offer apology. Had you not urged me to seek the truth, who knows how long I would have held on to all those negative feelings?"

Contentment had her sighing. She liked thinking that she'd helped Dakota put his demons to rest. Well, some of them, anyway.

"Will you stay?" he asked.

A tremulous feeling had her weak in the knees and she doubted her legs would have carried her back to the house had she wanted them to. But she didn't want them to. There wasn't another place she wanted to be more than right here, sitting on the cool grass next to Dakota.

"I'd love to."

His voice was rich, the ancient words he intoned

lyrical. His song reached down into the deepest depths of her, stirred her soul. The air, warmed by the dancing flames, opaque with smoke billowing heavenward, took on an acute reverence. Lyssa had never been a religious person, but a sense of sanctity seemed to envelope them. A purity that inspired her awe.

In that moment, she was instinctively sure that Dakota's mother not only heard his prayer, but forgave her son the error of his misplaced antagonism.

Also in that moment, Lyssa came to yet another solid conclusion. Here on Misty Glen Reservation was where she wanted to raise her child. Here in this beautiful place where peace abounded. Where life was slow and easy. Where a person could breathe, and feel free and unafraid.

Lyssa was gifted with a third and final piece of pure, unadulterated knowledge. The love she felt for the man sitting next to her was genuine, honest, sincere. True love that came directly from the heart.

The emotions that had spurred her first marriage had been shallow and self-serving. And it was no wonder that her egocentric actions had led her into nothing but a mess. But she was desperately trying to change that. She was a different person now. She cared. And she fully accepted responsibility for herself. For her ghastly choices. For her child.

With a baby to think about, she'd forced herself to see the superficiality of the life she'd created back in California. And she also saw that that existence just might psychologically harm her son or daughter. Dakota had helped her become brave enough to stop running, to stand strong, and face it all. And for that, she'd be forever in his debt.

The love she felt for him might never be returned. But right at this most sacred moment while the two of them sat together before the ceremonial fire, that didn't seem to matter.

What mattered was the joy that filled Lyssa, that had her smiling and feeling peaceful. Content.

That was what she wanted for her child. That was what she intended to provide for her baby. And no one—not Rodney with his harassment and intimidation, not the entire Gaines family—could keep her from it.

~oOo~

The next day, Dakota was hiking his way around Misty Lake even before the sun had risen. He carried a pack of medical supplies and nonperishable foodstuffs. He was on a mission.

The person he intended to visit probably would not be happy to see him, but his conscience wouldn't allow him to wait one day longer to make this trip into the mountains. The cabin couldn't be far now, Dakota surmised. It had been years since he'd visited the hunting lodge, the last time being when he was probably thirteen or fourteen. He smiled at the memories of the rowdy times he'd spent—

A flurry of movement on the path directly in front of him made him jump nearly out of his skin.

"Chay!" he shouted, adrenaline pumping. "Damn it! Do you have to hurl yourself on me like that?"

His cousin laughed. "You're crashing around like a wild bull out here. Any good Indian could hear you coming for miles."

Slightly embarrassed at having been caught off guard, Dakota continued his hike. "Yeah, well, there's not much call for creeping unnoticed into the enemy's camp these days."

"That's good," Chay wisecracked, falling into step beside him, "because you'd have been taken prisoner an hour ago."

"You've been tracking me for an hour? Geez, cuz—" he shrugged his way out of the backpack "—the least you could have done is offered to carry my pack for a while." He handed it over. "They're for you, by the way. Medical supplies and some canned goods. Mat thought you could use them."

"That lousy, no-good brother of yours never could keep a secret."

"He thought you might need some medical attention," Dakota told his cousin, shaking his head at the scowl Chay leveled on him. He knew his cousin's bark was worse than his bite. "And someone to talk to."

Like Dakota, Chay wore his hair long. His cousin's jeans were worn, his hiking boots dusty, but Dakota could clearly see that Chay was physically fit. However, something dark clouded Chay's onyx gaze.

A small log cabin came into view and Dakota continued to trudge toward it.

"The body is fine," his cousin finally replied. His

frown darkened further as he added, "It's the mind that's unsettled."

Neither man spoke until they reached the front porch. Dakota felt winded as he climbed the few steps and flopped down on the top tread. Working in an office day in and day out was making him soft.

"Did Mat tell Grandfather I'm here?" Chay queried.

Dakota shook his head. "He wouldn't break your confidence to that degree. But you should come down. See him. He'd be hurt to think you've been here, what—it's been weeks, Mat said—yet you haven't come to the rez."

A gloominess seemed to fall over Chay's countenance. "I need to be alone. Besides, I'm afraid our grandfather just may be part of my problem."

Something in Chay's tone kept Dakota from inquiring further about his cousin's odd comment.

"I'll come for a visit," Chay assured him. "When I'm ready."

Softly, Dakota probed, "Is there anything I can do to help?"

"There's not anything anyone can do. I need to work this out for myself."

As if he couldn't stand to be still another second, Chay stood and made for the door.

"Come on in and have a drink," he told Dakota. "Tell me what's been happening in your world. That'll take my mind off my own troubles for a while."

When the two men were seated inside the tiny one-room cabin, cups of cool spring water cradled between their hands, Chay whistled low and long once Dakota recounted the past few weeks.

"You got married? And quick, too. Do you love her?"

"Not just no, but hell no," Dakota shot back. "Absolutely not. She's helping me. And I'm helping her. And that's all there is to it."

But even as he spoke the words, he had to wonder if he might be lying through his teeth. Before he could think about it too closely, he told his cousin a bit about Lyssa's situation. Again, Chay whistled.

"And you think someone like this Gaines," Chay said, "who's used to having things his own way, is going to give up on a beautiful woman who just happens to be carrying his child?"

Dakota set down his empty cup and scrubbed at

his face. "I don't know." He sighed and rested his elbows on his knees. "But I intend to help Lyssa get out of this. She deserves a fresh start. I don't care what lengths I have to go to to see that she gets it."

His cousin's eyebrows rose a fraction. "And you're still going to hold on to the notion that this woman means nothing to you?"

"I never said that." Dakota heard the flint sharpness in his tone. "She means something."

She means a lot, a silent voice boldly inserted. Maybe too much.

Shoving the thought—and the sudden confusion that walloped him—right out of his mind, he continued, "She's done a lot for me, Chay. She's helped me to come to terms with... some things I've been grappling with. She's made it possible for me to get my head straight about the past."

His cousin remained silent, and Dakota got the distinct impression that the man he'd grown up with wasn't so sure he agreed that Dakota's head was straight about Lyssa and his feelings for her. Unfortunately, there was a light in his cousin's eye that suggested he just might push the matter. Before he could, Dakota rose from the chair.

"Listen, I need to get back." His chuckle was forced. "I have a medical practice to run. Patients to see."

Chay got up. "Thanks for the supplies."

The men hugged, and then Dakota leveled his gaze on his cousin. "Come down to the rez, Chay. Grandfather would love to see you."

"I will," Chay said. "As soon as I'm ready."

Dakota only nodded.

He paused on the porch and looked out at the trees and the lake. The serenity of the fall day was so at odds with the chaos Chay had stirred inside him with his questions regarding Lyssa and what she meant to him. He went down the steps and headed for the path that would take him back to the rez.

Back to Lyssa.

The thought came like a bolt of lightning from the sky and jolted his emotions into a total muddle. Thankful for the long trek home, he knew he had a lot of thinking to do.

CHAPTER NINE

Lyssa was sure she'd never laughed so much in her life. Even now her cheek muscles ached, but it was a good kind of pain.

Not one, but two patients had canceled their appointments late that afternoon, so Dakota had decided to close the office early. Then he'd done the most extraordinary thing. He'd asked her to go out to Misty Lake with him. And her acceptance of the invitation had been lightning quick.

The treetops were painted in the vibrant colors of fall: crimson and gold, bronze and amber. There was a chill in the air that forced them to bundle up in thick sweaters and gloves, but the sun was radiant, its beams warming and bright in the crystal-blue sky.

She'd never seen Dakota so carefree. Letting go of the anger he'd felt toward his mother had transformed him. Like a caterpillar metamorphosing into a dazzling butterfly, he'd gone from being sedate and serious to acting downright silly at times. Lyssa loved the change she saw in him.

Oh, he was still earnest when it came to his work. Treating his patients, helping to make them well, was his life's calling, that much was plain. But it was nice seeing him smile so easily, seeing him ready to have a little fun.

"So," he said, his tone full of mischief, "have you ever taken a swim in October?"

He leaned from one side to the other, rocking the small rowboat they'd taken out onto the glassy surface of the lake.

"Dakota!" Her squeal was both panicky and delighted as she grasped the sides of the boat and held on tightly. "Stop that right now."

The boat continued to undulate even after he halted his jerky motion. When his laughter faded, he dipped his chin, his eyes twinkling with merriment and some other emotion, some deeply powerful yet unnameable feeling that coursed throughout her.

"I haven't had this much fun in..." He cocked his head, silently calculating. Finally, he gave a tiny shrug. "I can't remember how long it's been."

The oars thumped the sides of the boat as he secured them in place. Then he clasped his hands together with a sigh. "I feel good," he told her. "Really good."

Lyssa's heart soared, marveling that she'd thought the very same thing only an instant before. "I'm glad."

His green eyes were on her again. "I have you to thank, you know."

Her smile widened. "You've already thanked me."

There was nothing awkward in the silence that fell between them.

That was another thing Lyssa had noticed. The discomfort that, in the not-too-distant past, had their eyes averting, that had them avoiding one another, had seemed to dissipate like clouds blown beyond the horizon by a stiff wind.

Oh, the awareness was still there. That amazing attraction. Oh, boy, was it ever still there! Her heart thudded and her blood heated every time he got anywhere near her. But being with him was easier now. Being with Dakota was comfortable. She noticed more and more that she felt happy. That, too, was nice.

Sensing his eyes on her again, she smiled.

"You look radiant."

His voice was soft and rich, and Lyssa felt pleasure shudder along her spine. She was about to thank him for the compliment, but before she could, he continued.

"People say that all pregnant women just glow," he said. "But don't you believe it. I've seen more than my share of females who are expecting. The majority of them look pasty and bloated."

She didn't know if he was being blatantly honest, or if he was simply attempting to make her feel good about the condition of her body.

"I'm surprised at you," she chastised, unable to hold back her chuckle. "You shouldn't talk like that about your pregnant patients. What would they think? Besides, you just give me time. I'm swelling up more every day. Soon my ankles will be as big around as my calves."

"Never!"

Dakota reached down, scooped up her foot by the heel, and placed it on his knee. Lyssa's eyes went round with surprise. He slipped off her shoe and she immediately felt the warmth of his palm smooth over the bridge of her stockinged foot.

"Not as long as I'm your doctor," he proclaimed.

His thumbs massaged her arch, and it felt so delicious that she closed her eyes and simply enjoyed the decadent treatment.

"That's nice," she murmured. "Mmm. So nice."

Nice was a word that floated around in her head a lot these days.

As Dakota rubbed her foot, Lyssa let her body relax, and listened to the birds chirping, the sound of the water lapping against the sides of the boat.

Nice.

She wouldn't mind it at all if life continued along like this indefinitely. No, she sure wouldn't mind.

"Do you ever think about it?" he asked.

Raising her eyelids, Lyssa looked into his handsome face.

"What having a baby will be like, I mean," he clarified. "How a child will change your life."

"I think about it all the time. In fact, the thought is never far from my mind."

Dakota said, "I've read that we learn parenting skills from our own mothers and fathers. I remember my parents. Vaguely. I'll be forever grateful for the depth of love they showered on me." Quietly, he added, "Even though I didn't even understand the magnitude of it at the time."

Although he hadn't told Lyssa all the details of his past, it was clear that he was at peace about it, and that pleased her to no end.

"But if I ever do become a father," Dakota continued, "if I ever do get the chance to see if I have a knack for parenting, it'll be my grandfather I'll model myself after. He was great to me, my brother, and my cousins. Just wonderful. Full of wisdom and patience."

Lyssa liked hearing him speak of the good memories of his childhood.

"Oh, Grandfather disciplined us when we needed it," he told her. "But for the most part, what I remember was that he loved us. And was proud of us. And he didn't hesitate to show us exactly how he felt."

The massaging motion of his fingers on her foot

stopped suddenly, and Lyssa could see that he was deep in thought.

Softly he declared, "That's the kind of father I want to be. Open with my feelings. Free with my love. I think kids can survive anything if they know they're loved, don't you?"

She didn't answer verbally. She only smiled.

It was impossible for her to keep from thinking of her own lonely childhood. The places she'd been forced to live, the moving around, the constant worry about what she'd eat or how she'd acquire clothing or supplies for school. She'd felt isolated and at a distinct disadvantage.

There had been nothing wonderful about her youth.

"What kind of mother do you think you'll make?"

Dakota's question aroused in her a huge doubt that sent her gaze drifting off across the lake. That very issue had filled her with fear ever since the day she'd discovered she was going to have a baby.

She'd had no real role model. Oh, her mother had been around some of the time, but the woman hadn't been much of a parent.

"I can't imagine loving my baby any more than I

do right now." She wasn't surprised to find that her hands had fluttered their way to her tummy. The smile tugging at the corners of her mouth was sad, though. "And I can tell you that I know what kind of parent I don't want to be."

She paused long enough to sigh. "I want my child to grow up happy, Dakota. And well cared for. I want my baby to always have a warm bed to sleep in, and good, nourishing food to eat. And I want to be there to hold him. And love him. And protect him." She lifted her eyes to his. "Whatever it is we have to face."

He smiled at her, resuming the massage, but Lyssa knew his mind wasn't really on the task of rubbing her foot.

"I guess," she felt compelled to add, "I'll just have to wing it."

Seemingly without thought, Dakota's hand slid upward and came to rest on her ankle. Heat spread up her leg in concentric waves and her breath caught and held.

"When it comes right down to it, that's exactly what most parents do, I would guess," he said.

He seemed not to notice what his touch was doing to her.

"Funny, isn't it?" he continued. "Parenting has to be the single most important duty a person can undertake, yet no training is offered. No formal education is available for the average person on how to care for children."

As he talked, his fingertips lingered beneath her trouser hem, slowly, inexplicably trailing to her Achilles' tendon, then higher still, caressing the sensitive skin low on the back of her calf. Even though autumn chilled the mountain air, she felt flushed, uncomfortably warm as the embers of desire smoldered inside her.

He seemed to realize suddenly that she hadn't responded to anything he'd said. His chuckle faded, his words died as he became cognizant of what was simmering between them out there on the glassy water.

In an instant, it seemed that the wind had been knocked out of him. His gaze locked with hers, fervor burning like white flames. His wide mouth parted, his tongue inadvertently skittering across his bottom lip. Lyssa fought the urge to loosen her sweater and she wouldn't have been the least surprised if the lake began to seethe and simmer and set the boat pitching to and fro from the heat of this sudden, all-consuming ardor.

His mouth formed soundless words. His fingers stilled on her calf. Time halted.

Finally, he blinked. Swallowed. Inhaled deeply. And with what seemed a firm deliberateness he released his hold on her foot, guiding it back down to the floor of the rowboat.

"We should get back," he said, his voice raspy. He fumbled for the oars, giving the chore much more attention than it deserved.

Lyssa should have felt discomfited. Once again the two of them had been taken unawares by that amazing allure. However, she didn't feel the least bit ill at ease, even though that was clearly what Dakota suffered. Strangely, what she was battling was the urge to smile big and broad. She sensed that, for the first time, Dakota wasn't out and out rejecting the attraction that pulsed between them. Instead, she got the impression that his reaction was more like... contemplation. As if he were wrestling with the idea of what it might mean were they to allow themselves to explore this astounding passion bubbling just below the surface.

She'd been there, done that. And joy burst inside her to observe that he might finally be reaching that point, too.

He put all his concentration into rowing them back to shore, and Lyssa didn't break the silence. She understood that he needed the quiet. Needed this time to reflect and sort through what he was feeling.

Lyssa spied the sleek black limousine long before they reached the shore. The sunshine glinted blindingly off the shiny chrome bumper, the tinted glass, even the fancy ornament on the hood, and her chest filled with a heavy dread.

"He's back," she whispered. "Rodney's back."

Dakota took a moment to look over his shoulder, but he went right back to propelling the boat toward the small dock.

There was great strength in his green eyes when he looked at her.

"It's okay," he said softly. "He can't hurt you."

"I know. But he can make trouble for me." Worry bit into her forehead. "And everyone around me. Lots of trouble. And he'll enjoy doing it." Her anxiety hitched up a notch as she admitted, "I'm terrified that he'll use his fortune to somehow secure custody of our child."

There. It was out. The greatest fear weighing her down.

"There's no way we'll let that happen. I have a cousin, Tristin. He's a lawyer. A good one. He'll be happy to help us, I'm sure."

Even though trepidation had her feeling quaky inside, she smiled. The way he'd phrased his comments was palpable confirmation that he was with her in this. Even though he knew the opponent to be both wealthy and powerful.

She wasn't alone in this mess. And that meant a lot. A whole lot.

Her fingers where shaking as she looped the lanyard over the docking post. Dakota got out of the boat and then held his hand out to steady her exit. She wasn't surprised—and felt terribly grateful—when he didn't break contact with her, holding tightly to her hand as they closed the gap between them and the trouble that lay ahead.

Rodney was getting out of the back seat of the car as she and Dakota set foot on the lakeshore.

"I've come to take you home." Her ex-husband's tone was resolute, his eyes hard as steel.

Her instinct was to wither, but Dakota put gentle pressure on her hand as assurance and promise that all would be just fine.

Tipping up her chin, she said, "I am home. I told you that the last time you came. I'm not going back to California. I'm staying right here." Feeling the need of a good verbal punch, she firmly added, "With my husband."

"Why would you want that—" he indicated Dakota with a small, dismissing toss of his head, his words smooth "—when I can give you everything your heart desires?"

"What you give," she told him, "comes with too high a price."

Rodney shrugged. "Everything has a price, Lyssa. Everything. I'll bet what you think you have now... with him... came with a price, as well."

Lyssa's insides shrank. Her marriage to Dakota *had* come with a price. Their relationship had started out as a mutual give-and-take. But that had changed sometime over the past several weeks. She'd gained a trusted friend in Dakota. She'd lost her heart to him. She'd discovered the true meaning of love.

"I won't let you denigrate what Dakota and I

have," she said boldly. "Because of him I now know about devotion. About loyalty. Love is wanting your mate to be happy, even when things aren't going the way you'd like."

Shock jolted through her and her eyes went wide when she heard the silent implications in her statement. She couldn't bring herself to look at Dakota.

Under his breath, Rodney murmured, "That's the biggest bunch of bull I've ever heard."

His rude proclamation offended her. "For some odd reason, Rodney, your attitude doesn't surprise me."

His jaw tensed so tightly it looked painful.

"Lyssa," he said curtly, "I think I've been more than patient here. You're carrying my baby. You ran off and hooked up with the first man you found. And you did it all without giving me any warning. Your objective has been successful. You got my attention. You've stirred my jealousy. Now—"

"You are the most arrogant man I have ever met!"

She pulled her hand from Dakota's, balling her fingers into tight fists. "I did not run off to get your attention. I was not intending to make you jealous. Dakota and I are not merely 'hooked up.' We're married, Rodney. Married. And that makes me unavailable to you."

"You'll never be unavailable to me, Lyssa. Never."

There was a coaxing—an assuredness—in his tone that told Lyssa this man honestly felt he could acquire anything he wanted. Fury exploded in her head like glowing red fireworks.

"We're connected," he said, his entire demeanor as smooth as the shiny black finish on the limousine he stood next to. "That baby you're carrying will connect us forever." He smiled, charm oozing from every pore. "You can't get away from me. And I'll soon have you admitting that you really never wanted that to begin with."

Evidently, he thought he was making progress, because his smile was sugary sweet.

"You got confused is all, honey," he crooned. "You just got a little mixed up. You're mine, Lyssa. You'll always be mine."

Her only thought was to pummel that smarmy grin right off his face, but when she made to move toward him, Dakota stopped her with a firm hand on her arm. She looked at him and his expression spoke volumes.

As she studied his face, a calmness came over her. She felt so indebted to this man. He'd remained silent, allowing her to fight her own battle. But the moment he saw that she was losing control, that anger was urging her to do something she'd regret, he'd stepped in to help.

She offered him the smallest of smiles, hoping he understood the gratitude she was feeling.

Finally, she felt calm enough to say, "I don't love you, Rodney. I never loved you. I only loved your money. I feel horrible that I did that to you. And I'm sorry. But that's just the way things are."

His laugh was hearty. "Don't feel badly about that, sweetheart," he told her. "I love my money, too. That doesn't mean we can't make this work."

Control slipped from her clumsy grasp once again. "No one is this thick!"

Something in her tone triggered Dakota to react. He turned his attention to Rodney, his body stance turning rigid. "This will stop. Now. Lyssa shouldn't be upset. It isn't good for her or the child."

Rodney leveled a smug look on Dakota, his chest

puffing in a buffoonish manner. "*My child.* That's my baby she's carrying."

Dakota said, "That fact has never been disputed."

"Good," the man said, emphasizing what he evidently thought was a triumph over the opposition. He directed his attention back onto Lyssa. "If you won't come home for us, then you will come home for the baby's sake."

Crossing her arms over her chest, she tipped up her chin mulishly. "I'll say it one more time. I'm not going anywhere."

"You'll come with me, damn it!"

Rodney took two steps toward her, but Dakota planted his body firmly in front of Lyssa. Her ex stopped dead in his tracks.

"You're getting ready to cross a line," Dakota ground out. "Think hard before you do."

It quickly became clear to her that it never entered Rodney's head that his efforts to take what he considered his would be thwarted, that Dakota might take things to a physical level. Frustration and anger and confusion as to what he should do next darkened his features. Finally, Rodney turned toward the car.

"Make her come home, Daddy," he called.

Lyssa reached up, covered her mouth with her fingers. Pity welled up in her when she heard the childish whine in Rodney's voice. She watched as the rear door opened on the far side of the car, and the senior Gaines stepped out of the limo.

Although he was small of stature, Lyssa knew that there wasn't a more formidable man in the California corporate world. Samuel Gaines had been the ruin of many a businessman. Now, though, his smile was warm and frighteningly friendly.

"Hello, Missy," he greeted Lyssa.

She cringed, feeling as if she'd walked, unawares, into a massive spider web. From the very first time she'd met Sam, he'd called the wives of all three of his sons Missy. Lyssa got the impression that either he couldn't bother to remember the names of his daughters-in-law, or he didn't feel they were worth having identities of their own.

He closed the door and rounded the rear of the car, stopping only when he'd reached Rodney's side.

"I wanted to give my boy here every opportunity

to solve his own problem." Sam clapped his hand on his son's shoulder.

Just a moment before, Rodney may have acted cocky, but at least he'd seemed to have a backbone. Now that he stood beside his father, his shoulders rounded, his face crumpled, the result made him look pathetic. Lyssa was amazed that there had been any amount of money that had made him look attractive to her. Guilt rushed at her and she hated thinking that she'd seen the solution to her childhood filled with poverty in the Gaines family fortune. Well, that was one blunder she was simply going to have to live with. At least she'd learned something from the experience. Something important. No amount of money could buy happiness.

"If there's one thing I've learned," Samuel said, stuffing his hands nonchalantly into the pockets of his trousers, "it's that everyone has a price. What's yours, Missy? What will it take for you to come home with us? A vacation villa in Italy? A yacht with all the trimmings? Hell, you name it, it's yours."

She stepped up beside Dakota. "I don't want anything you've got, Sam."

His friendly smile faded, the warning glistening in his eye meant to strike terror.

"It's not my practice to make an offer more than once. You turn me down and you'll be making the mistake of a lifetime."

"I already made that," Lyssa told him. "When I married your son. I don't love him, Sam. So I got out."

"Love." He bit out the word with disgust. "People put too much stock in mere emotion. Marriage is a business, pure and simple." His grin was scary. "You're in breach of contract, Missy."

She feared she might cry, but then Dakota reached over and slid his palm into hers. The strength that radiated from him was all she needed.

"I'm not going anywhere, and that's that. Don't bother suggesting it again." She looked at her ex. "I'm sorry if I hurt you, Rodney, but my mind's made up. There's no chance of us being together."

Silence hummed.

Finally, Samuel said, "Well, then. It sure does seem like that's that. So I guess you really do deserve what you're about to get."

Something in his tone made the small hairs on the back of Lyssa's neck stand on end, and she tried to no avail to stifle the cold fear that trickled down the full length of her spine one vertebra at a time.

The elder man turned to his son. "I'd hoped she'd do right by you, boy," he said, giving his shoulder a bolstering nudge. "For both her sake and for that of the child she's carrying. But it looks like she's not too concerned for your happiness."

He tossed Lyssa a scornful look, and in a flash his eyes turned granite hard. "I do have some information to help my boy deal with losing you. You're not worthy to be part of the Gaines family, Missy. I know where you come from. I know what you are."

Dread dried up Lyssa's throat until she felt as if someone had lighted a match and scorched the length of her esophagus. No. No! She wanted to scream.

"Your mama was a prostitute."

She watched in horror as her former father-in-law's mouth formed the words. But she felt as if she were hearing them from far off. She wished with all her heart that that's where she was hearing them... from miles and miles away from this place. However, luck had never been that good to her.

"She never even knew which one of her johns

knocked her up," he continued viciously. "You never knew your daddy, did you, Missy?"

The muscles making it possible for her to swallow were paralyzed. Moving, speaking, thinking... all of these things were impossible.

"You're the product of filth."

Lyssa wanted to bury her face in her hands, to hide herself from the truth. Rodney's pitiable posture transformed as he heard his father's diatribe. Her ex-husband's spine straightened and his face scrunched up into nothing short of revulsion.

The fact that both Gaines men were now looking down their noses at her bothered her not one whit. What killed her inside was knowing that Dakota was discovering the truth about her, that her past was filled with nothing but trashy lewdness.

"Why, it wouldn't surprise me in the least, boy," Samuel said to his son loudly, boldly, "if that baby in her belly isn't even yours."

"Damn, Daddy," Rodney whispered, "you're probably right." He raked Lyssa with a scathing look unmistakably articulating that the very sight of her nauseated him.

"Thank you, Daddy," he said to his father. "Thank you for saving me."

Samuel Gaines nodded. "That just goes to show you how much I love you, boy. And don't you forget it."

Without another word, without another glance her way, Rodney and his father got into the limousine and were driven out of Lyssa's life.

Dust kicked up by the car tires swirled in the air. She had the vague thought that she should be jumping up and down with joy. She was rid of Rodney and the whole Gaines family. Forever.

However, she was too humiliated by the disaster that Sam had left behind. She felt as if the man had torn her into shreds and had scattered the pieces all over the ground. She felt exposed. Mortified. And she couldn't bring herself to lift her eyes to Dakota.

Her heart was filled with love for him. From him she'd learned what dignity was all about. She respected his intelligence. His honor. The code by which he lived his life. She felt privileged to have had the opportunity to work with him. To be married to him.

But... a groan gathered in the back regions of her

throat... what must he think of her after learning what she was? What she came from?

She swallowed around the huge lump of emotion that had swelled in her throat and winced at the pain. After dragging in a lungful of air, she wrested her eyes from the ground and made herself look into his face.

His moss-green eyes were shadowed with a pity so immense, it was nearly tangible. Horrified beyond words, Lyssa felt hot tears rush and well and burn. Her chin trembled, and her heart splintered like shards of thin glass.

"Don't look at me like that!" she shouted. "*Don't you look at me like that!*"

Her sobs ripped through the warm autumnal air and the humiliation became more than she could endure. So she raced away from it all.

CHAPTER TEN

————————

The drawers in the chest were empty and Lyssa snapped the latches closed on her suitcase. Letting her eyes trip over the room, she saw the barren dresser top and nightstand. Her heart felt just as austere as the vacant room.

Once again, she felt like a rat scurrying from trouble.

Where will you go? What will you do for money? How will you ever provide for the baby?

The dark questions mocked her until she felt she wanted to scream.

She had no answers. She only knew she needed to leave here. Quickly. She couldn't face Dakota again. Couldn't stand to see the pity clouding his gorgeous green eyes.

Her heart ached like an abscessed tooth as she contemplated never seeing him again. Yet there was nothing else to be done. Living with the longing and love she felt for him would be her punishment. Maybe after a little suffering she'd finally learn that love had never been meant to be part of her destiny.

People like her—like her mother—existed on a constant diet of pain and anguish. Making one glorious blunder after another. Falling down, scraping knees and elbows, rising and brushing off, only to fall yet again. When would she realize that? When would she stop banging her head against a brick wall, trying to make her life better?

Folks who started out so low on the ladder of repute could never get a foothold to climb out of their miserable circumstance. There was always someone hovering above them just waiting to knock them back down.

She flattened her hand at the base of her throat. It was so unlike her to wallow in her shame and self-pity. She'd gone for months and months without obsessing over her mother's sins... the sins from which Lyssa herself had been born. She'd had such high hopes for a brighter tomorrow. But now those hopes were completely destroyed.

Then some strange light shined in her head, plucking at her attention, refusing to be ignored.

Hope? No, Lyssa couldn't bring herself to describe it as such.

Her mouth firmed with resolve when she identified what it was.

Responsibility.

No matter how pessimistic she felt about her own future right now, she had an obligation to continue on, pressing forward, maintaining that constant effort to change her situation.

"I'm sorry," she whispered, pressing her hand tightly against her belly. "I'll do better," she told her baby. "For you. And for me. We'll go somewhere new. Start over fresh. For us. I will make a better life for you, I promise."

She silently prayed that the optimism she attempted to inject into her tone belied the serious doubt that weighed so heavily on her shoulders.

Lyssa picked up her bag and left the bedroom. She was two feet away from the front door when she heard the key in the lock, saw Dakota enter.

Her heart stopped beating right then and there.

Getting out of the house before he returned had been her most heartfelt wish. But once again she found that it was futile to even consider that luck might be on her side. Why should fate grant her anything in this mess she'd made when it had been against her in everything else?

The hurt on his face was unmistakable.

"You were planning to leave without saying goodbye?"

Guilt. Oh, the guilt was more than she could bear.

This man had done so much for her over the past weeks since she'd arrived in New England. He'd helped her while knowing absolutely nothing about her. He'd given her time to heal without intruding in on her personal life with questions any normal person wouldn't have been able to keep silent about. She thought about the lovely nursery he'd surprised her with... a nursery her baby would never use. She thought about how he'd offered his skills as a physician to care for her during her pregnancy.

She closed her eyes. He was practically a saint.

And the lengths he'd gone to in order to shield

her! He'd married her, for goodness' sake. He'd stood up to her ex, not once but twice. He'd even faced off with the Gaines family patriarch.

She was a horrible person to repay him in this manner—running off without even a simple goodbye—after all the trouble he'd encountered for her.

"I was only attempting to make it easier," she told him, emotion grating against her dry throat, "for both of us."

He didn't look convinced.

She continued, "Now that Rodney is out of my life, there's no reason for me to take refuge here any longer, Dakota."

His intense gaze bore into her like laser beams. She wanted to run, to hide, to burrow under a rock like a bug. The fact that he knew all of her secrets devastated her. Unshed tears burned the backs of her eyelids, but she refused to cry. Enough of her weaknesses had been laid bare for him.

"I know you said you hate secrets," she said, "but I just couldn't bring myself to tell you... everything."

She wanted nothing more than to rush out the

front door, but she knew in her heart that she couldn't do it. He deserved an explanation.

"I loved my mother," she declared as boldly as was possible for her in this moment of utter humiliation. "I loved her very much. I was terribly ashamed of her... of her *career* choice. The one bone of contention between us was that she saw nothing wrong in making what she called 'easy money' by selling her body."

Lyssa bit her lip, but forced herself to continue.

"I hated that she was a prostitute. But she loved me. She was a good mother. She tried very hard to provide for me. Yes, she failed to supply the simple basic needs more times than she succeeded, but..."

Her shoulders rounded as her breath left her in a frustrated rush. Unable to understand her mother's mentality and motivations where making a living was concerned, even after all these years, Lyssa ran out of ways to try to explain to Dakota.

"I was determined not to follow in her footsteps," she told him. "I can't remember a time when I didn't have a job. Running errands for my mother's... friends. Mowing lawns. Shoveling snow. Bagging groceries. Anything to make a buck.

I saved every penny I could... to help out all I could."

The smile tugging at her mouth was small and sad. "In the end, I think my mother must have learned something from my determination to live right. She got a legitimate job." Her gaze averted to the floor as she became momentarily lost in memories. "Not that she was ever happy about it. She was forever complaining that her 'real' job paid less money for much more work." Memories of her mother made her heart ache. "But knowing that she wanted to make me proud—to give up what she knew I saw as sordid—has to be worth *something*, doesn't it?"

Her voice softened as she repeated, "That has to be worth something."

The last bit of the story was heart-wrenching. Lyssa moistened her cracked lips and pressed toward the end. "I am so happy—" her quivering chin was in direct contradiction to her words "—that she and I had such a wonderful relationship in the end... right up until she died... from complications of a sexually transmitted disease."

Some people might say that, for someone like

her mother, that was simply just rewards. But not Lyssa. She wouldn't wish that kind of suffering on anyone.

She swallowed her pain. Now was the time for leaving behind the past and moving on. Squaring her shoulders, she forced herself to look Dakota in the eye. And that was a hard thing, knowing that the skeletons in her closet had been brought out into the bright sunshine for him to view... and judge.

Hurt continued to tense his beautiful face, as his shoulders rounded with what she could only imagine was disappointment. Well, he could just join the club. She was as disappointed in her life—*in herself*—as he appeared to be.

"I saw the disgust and the loathing in Rodney's eyes," she told him. "And I saw the pity in yours. I can't live with that. I'm going away, Dakota. Someplace where no one knows about my past. I need to start over." She shook her head. "Not just for me, but for my baby's sake."

Her breath hitched in her chest. "I've got to go, Dakota."

She pushed her way past him. If she didn't leave this instant, she just might start sobbing, ask for his forgiveness and beg him to love her as much as she loved him. However, the idea of facing humiliation on that grand scale was absolutely overwhelming.

"I've got to go," she repeated on her way out the door for no one's benefit but her own. "Now!"

~oOo~

"I don't understand why she didn't tell me," Dakota said, pacing the length of the living room.

He'd spent hours trying to sort through his feelings on his own. His failure to do so had him seeking out the wisest man he knew: his grandfather.

"I've done nothing," he said, agitation driving his fingers through his hair, "but show Lyssa that I'm worthy of her trust."

Grayson sat quietly listening.

"I could have handled the truth. I proved to her, over and over again, that she could rely on me. I just don't understand. Why would she not tell me?" He lifted both his shoulders and his palms in frustration. "She said she remembered my saying that I don't like secrets. And maybe I did. But what I remember saying was that I don't like lies and manipulation. She didn't lie to me. She didn't try to manipulate me. Why would she think that I couldn't handle the truth about her past? Especially when her past isn't all that bad. Okay, so her mother chose to work in a vocation that was... a little out of the ordinary. That has no bearing on Lyssa. None whatsoever."

The air became very still, and when Dakota realized he'd been asking dozens of questions without giving his grandfather a chance to reply, he paused. Then he did what he knew was necessary if he were to receive any answers. He calmed his restless spirit, and then he went and sat down in the chair that placed him face-to-face with the astute shaman.

When Grayson smiled, his face grew even more craggy, his eyes softening. "My son," he began gently, "as much as you want this to be about you and how you've been misjudged by Lyssa, I must tell you this has nothing whatsoever to do with you."

Dakota would be lying if he said he didn't feel irritated. He'd come here seeking vindication. He'd come here wanting to have his hurt feelings validated.

"This is all about seasons," the old man pronounced.

The bewilderment that rushed over Dakota had him frowning and he didn't bother to hide his impatience for Grayson to explain his strange decree.

"Two people can look at the same object," the shaman continued, "yet see two entirely different things. Take a tree, for instance. You might see a bounty of leaves, green and fanning in the summer breeze. Where Lyssa might see bare branches that resemble claws reaching up toward the stark clouds of winter."

Finally, Dakota shook his head. "I know you're trying to teach me something here, but I don't understand what you're saying."

"Seasons, my son." Grayson clasped his knurled hands together in his lap. "Lyssa has lived with her past for many years. She's had many seasons to build up her fears about who she is and how she is received. She's had a lot of time, experienced many circumstances, good and bad. And I predict most of them pertaining to her past have been bad."

And then he locked eyes with Dakota as he

explained, "She is simply looking at the tree from the season in which she exists."

The old man fell silent, giving Dakota time to assimilate all that had been said.

Absently, Dakota's fingers ran over his jaw, pinched his chin, traced his own lips. Soon his frustration was overwhelmed with a new anxiety.

"Oh, sweet heaven, Grandfather!" He felt his throat close with panic. "I love her. I don't give a damn where she came from! I want her here. With me."

He wasn't all that surprised by the outburst. There had been a battle raging in him for some time now. His feelings for Lyssa had been growing by the hour... by the minute. And those emotions had been warring with his stubborn determination to protect his heart from being broken.

But today, out on the lake, the allure that entwined him and Lyssa had been unmistakable. Undeniable. And at first he'd felt the urge to panic. But as he'd rowed the boat toward shore, he saw the emotion for what it really was.

Love.

In his mind's eye, he'd watched as his feelings for Lyssa had weaved themselves into an intricate pattern. A bolt of richly textured fabric that rolled itself out before him... into the future. *Their future.*

He'd just been about to confide these thoughts to her when she'd alerted him that her ex-husband was waiting on shore.

"I love her," he repeated the three small words. "But now I feel as if I've lost her... all because of my own stubbornness."

"Then go find her," Grayson advised.

"But—" anxiety welled up in him "—I stood there feeling hurt the whole time she was confessing her past. I should have reassured her. But all I did was stagger around in my own wounded emotions. My behavior was unforgivable."

His grandfather's lips pursed. Then he said, "You'll never find out for sure until you go seek forgiveness."

~oOo~

"My life was a mess when you took me in," Lyssa said, fresh tears spilling heedlessly down her pale cheeks. "You try to help me get sorted, but I succeeded in turning things into a complete disaster again. If you don't want me staying here, I'll understand."

Tori Landing brought two mugs of steaming herbal tea to the couch where Lyssa sat curled into a ball, her knees bent, her heels pressed to the backs of her thighs.

"Don't be silly," Tori crooned. "You're welcome to stay just as long as you need to."

Lyssa had arrived at Freedom Trail, Tori's B&B, hours ago. The two women had sat together, Tori listening, Lyssa crying and blubbering as she did her best to explain everything.

Once Lyssa had calmed down, her friend had attempted to get her to eat, but Lyssa had no appetite.

Dusk fell early in the New England autumn, and tonight the air was laced with a nip that clearly announced winter wasn't far off. Lyssa felt chilled to the bone. Even the fire Tori had built in the large hearth hadn't done much to stop her shivering. She knew it was more nerves than anything else.

"I'll never get over that sight," Lyssa told Tori yet again. "Rodney's father announced to the whole world that my mother was a whore, and the pity pulsed off Dakota in waves. I could feel it, I tell you."

Tori cradled the mug between her hands. "I understand. A scene like that would be distressing to anyone. But I don't want you to worry. There are other jobs out there. Other doctors in need of a nurse. There are hospitals, nursing homes. We'll start looking right away."

Her friend's assurance that she could easily find gainful employment did little to lift her spirits, and evidently discerning that there was more to Lyssa's agony than merely the loss of a job, Tori gasped and set down her tea on the coffee table.

"Oh, honey," the woman said. "Can you ever forgive me? I didn't realize." Then she took Lyssa's hand. "You love him."

Lyssa's heart broke along with her voice as she answered, "Yes. I do." A tear slipped silently down her face. "Tori, I feel like I've loved him all my life."

The two women shared a moment of silence.

"I know that's crazy," Lyssa continued. "B-but that's exactly how I feel. As if he's been a part of me forever."

Patting her hand, Tori said, "It's not crazy. Not at

all. Don't you think every woman wishes she could meet a man who makes her feel like that?"

Tori picked up Lyssa's mug and pressed it into her palms. "Hold on to this, honey. You're chilled to the bone."

"I've wished so hard that I could take it all back. Do things all over again. If I had met Dakota years ago, I would never have made the mistakes I made. The love I have for him would have helped me to see things clearly. Would have lighted my way and kept me from botching things up so badly."

"Don't ever wish away the past," Tori said. "It's made you who you are. If you didn't survive your failed marriage, if you didn't try so hard to make a second go of it and suffer through that failure, why, who knows? You might not have recognized Dakota as the blessing he is. You might never have fallen in love with him so deeply."

Lyssa sat there, ruminating on the truths her friend was revealing. Her own thinking had been so shallow in her early years. All she'd thought about was surviving economically. Matters of the heart weren't of much significance. There was no way Dakota would have found that attractive. Not after what he'd experienced with his ex-wife. But

Tori was right. She probably wouldn't have appreciated Dakota had she not had to suffer through living with Rodney. And had she not felt forced into fleeing California, she'd have never contacted the abused women's group that had put her in contact with Tori; Lyssa would never have moved to Vermont.

Tori stared into the fire before commenting further on the topic at hand. "To feel that depth of emotion, even for just a few weeks, would be more than some women could ever wish for."

Lyssa felt the heat seeping through the ceramic mug, suddenly realizing that Tori's special and secretive work here at the B&B must keep her feeling isolated. Alone and lonely.

Finally, she felt compelled to say, "I'm sorry, Tori. For leaning on you so heavily. I should pull myself up by my own bootstraps, I know. I should be stronger. I'm going to have to be, if my child is ever going to be able to rely on me."

"Oh, now—" Tori tossed her a gentle smile "—stop being so hard on yourself. And you don't need to apologize to me. I'm your friend. And being around when you're needed is exactly what friends are for, right?"

Lyssa could only give a silent nod. And as she sat there sipping tea in Tori's warm and welcoming living room, she took a moment to send up a silent prayer that her friend's seclusion might be broken. She had no idea how or when or from where an answer might come, she only knew Tori deserved a man of her own. A saving kind of love.

The women talked for quite some time. Finally it seemed that Tori could hold back her yawn no longer.

"I'd better get to bed," she told Lyssa. "I have guests arriving early tomorrow." She grinned. "Real vacationers who expect to be pampered at my quaint little bed-and-breakfast."

Worry nibbled at Lyssa's mind. "Will I be in the way?"

Tori shook her head vehemently. "No. This house is big enough to accommodate all of us." She reached up and tucked a wayward strand of her hair behind her ear. "But this situation does give me one more reason for that cottage I've been wanting."

"A cottage?"

"Yes," Tori said. "I've been thinking of having that old carriage house out back renovated into a little hideaway. Someplace where my special guests can have some privacy."

"That sounds like a wonderful idea," Lyssa breathed. "But I don't want you to worry about me. I promise to put on a brave face for your guests. I won't spoil their vacation with my melancholy."

Tori only smiled. "I know you won't."

Just then the evocative sound of a rich, deep timbre made both of them go completely still.

"What on earth..." Tori went to the front window and peered out into the darkness.

That voice was all too familiar to Lyssa. It was the same song she'd heard before. She couldn't understand the words, but she knew who was doing the singing. Her heart pounded like a hammer against her ribs, and where just a moment ago she felt chilled to the marrow, she now felt flushed with a mingling of curiosity and panic.

She'd thought she was finished with trying to cope with the man she'd grown to love. The man she couldn't have. Not to mention his all-too-thorough knowledge of her shameful past.

Tori bustled from the windows flanking the front of the house to the ones facing the back. She turned rounded eyes onto Lyssa.

"It's Dakota," she whispered.

But Lyssa hadn't needed that information.

Spying between the curtain seams at the scene unfolding out in the backyard, Tori said, "And it looks as if he's... well, I can't really say for certain, but it seems that he's... praying."

This time when Tori directed her gaze at Lyssa, the woman's eyebrows were knitted with puzzlement.

"Why would he...?" The remainder of Tori's question was left unasked as something akin to enlightenment glittered in her eyes. A small smile played around the corners of her mouth.

"I'm going to bed," she announced suddenly to Lyssa. "I have a strong feeling you're going to need a little privacy. But before I go—" she retrieved a thick wool cardigan that had been hanging in the closet "—I want you to take this outside with you when you go. It's chilly out there."

"I'm not going out there." Lyssa heard the stress in her voice.

Tori didn't argue, she simply draped the sweater over the back of nearby chair.

Dakota's singing continued and Lyssa's panic

flared into alarm. The chanting was a clear invitation. But she wasn't going out there.

While her mind engaged in the taciturn debate, Tori had slipped out of the room, leaving Lyssa all too aware that she really was ultimately on her own. Her feet felt heavy with dread as she set down her mug of tea, picked up the cozy sweater, and made her way to the French doors that led out to the deck.

His words sure sounded a lot like the prayers he'd sung when he'd made atonements for having judged his mother so harshly. Only this song had a distinctively joyous ring to it.

The man was probably thanking his lucky stars he was rid of her!

But why perform his ceremony here? Why prolong the agony of their parting any further? Well, she'd never discover the answers standing here inside the house when he was out there on the lawn.

Light from the living room shafted into the darkness, casting her long shadow across the wooden deck and onto the grass where Dakota sat cross-legged, his arms extended to the heavens, his long blue-black hair spilling down his back, across his shoulders.

A strange heated chill coursed over her. He was so beautiful. So utterly beautiful.

She realized that, although he was once again speaking in his native language, whatever ritual he was enveloped in—whatever ceremony had him swathed in that amazing and mysterious aura of spiritual grace—was slightly different from the prayer song she'd witnessed before. For one, there was no fire. And secondly, he was fully clothed—the memory of seeing his corded bare chest glowing bronze in the firelight flashed in her mind and caused a heated desire to bud to life deep inside her. The agony of wanting what she couldn't have had a powerful regret soughing through her anew.

Suffering with this oh-too-pleasant pain would be the bane of her existence. For all eternity.

She stepped out onto the deck, closed the door behind her and went to stand at the railing. The Algonquian words Dakota sang were lush and harmonious. His song was calming. Curing.

The man was a true healer. In every sense of the word.

Silently, she slipped her arms into the sweater, tucking it securely around her, and then settled in to listen.

Too quickly, it seemed, Dakota fell silent, his arms lowering to his sides. But his eyes remained closed, his chin tipped high, his torso expanding as he took a deep breath. Lyssa got the distinct impression that he was reluctant to depart from this mystical haze that spiraled and swirled like glowing forest wraiths dancing around him on the night air.

Finally, he leveled his head—and his gaze zeroed in on her. She reached out and curled her fingers over the smooth railing for support. He rose to a stand in one fluid motion, emphasizing the force in his jean-clad muscular thighs. Like a hawk homing in on prey, Dakota trekked toward her.

Helplessly, she found herself admitting, "That was beautiful."

"It was a demonstration of thanksgiving."

Ah, so he was thanking his lucky stars he was rid—

"I was praising The Great One for bringing the woman of my heart into my life," he said, pausing at the bottom step.

She stood there, breathless, silent.

"I was also sending up prayers of gratitude that I was able to find you before you left Misty Glen altogether."

He reached his hand out to her, palm up.

Lyssa stared at his tawny fingertips, fear gripping her. She shook her head, whispering, "I can't. I just can't."

"Trust me, Lyssa." His jaw tightened, his hand lowered as he admitted, "A very wise man told me this isn't about me. You see, I nearly got lost in feeling hurt by the fact that you don't seem to have much confidence in me. Even after all that we'd been through together." He paused. "But Grandfather helped me to realize it's not me you distrust. It's your experiences. You've suffered through a lot, Lyssa. And the manner in which you've been treated in the past has you feeling doubtful and suspicious."

He moistened his lips, and Lyssa's gaze riveted on the path of his tongue.

"What I'm asking of you now," he continued, "is to put aside all your negative feelings. To judge me only on what you've experienced—since we met." Again, he reached out his hand to her. "If you don't," he added, his tone brimming with earnest emotion, "I fear we're going to be missing out on something spectacular. Something that was meant to be."

Her thoughts and feelings ran riot. Her insides trembled with trepidation. Tainted by a past so ugly she'd strived desperately to keep it hidden from everyone around her, Lyssa felt terrified that Dakota hadn't thought of all the ramifications involved in his offering to—

Heck, she didn't even know what it was he was offering!

Something that was meant to be. His words echoed through her mind.

She looked at this man whose face was so striking it could steal her breath away, and she couldn't help but thank the good Lord above that he wanted anything at all to do with her after learning about her past.

Whatever it was he was seeking... whatever he was offering, Lyssa felt that the "spectacular something" he'd mentioned was well worth the risk he was asking her to take.

Slowly, deliberately, she lifted her hand and slid

her fingers into his warm palm. He gripped hers firmly, and Lyssa found it freeing. And secure.

His smile was so bright, she was surprised that it didn't light up the night.

He led her down the stairs, and the two of them turned to face the mountains. The thick forest was majestic, a formidable presence against the backdrop of the starry sky. Moonlight dusted the scene with a radiant glow.

Dakota guided her along and she didn't give a single thought about where he might be leading her. She'd have followed him anywhere.

However, no amount of sanctuary could have curbed the anxiety from tumbling off her tongue. "I'm afraid. I'm fighting the urge to run. I-I'm afraid you're going to be sorry that you—"

"Shh," he hushed her. "The time for running has been over ever since you arrived here. One thing you can be sure of, Lyssa. I'll never be sorry for anything we've had."

He led her into a tiny garden area, urged her to sit on the bench.

"I have something I want to tell you," he said. He eased himself down beside her. "It's important that you know why I'll never be sorry... That I'll be forever grateful. To you."

Lyssa allowed the confusion she felt to express itself on her face. Softly, she asked, "How could you feel grateful toward me, Dakota? All I've done is bring one big fat mess after another for you to deal with."

"Oh, no," he disagreed. "You helped, Lyssa. In a way no one else could. I'm talking about the fact that you urged me to find out the truth about my past. About my mother. About my biological father."

He hadn't told her much about his discovery, but she did understand he'd found some solace. That the answers he'd received had given him some peace.

"You see," he continued, "the fact that neither of us knew our biological fathers was a commonality between us." He frowned. "But the only offense your father made was that he paid for sex." He paused long enough to sigh. He looked into her face, his gaze penetrating. "Mine was a rapist."

Lyssa felt the color drain from her face. Reaching up, she placed gentle fingers on his cheek.

"Oh, Dakota, I'm so sorry. Your poor mother."

She swallowed, looked away, let her hand fall to her lap, and then lifted her eyes to his. "I-I don't know what to say."

He told her all that he had discovered, and she was amazed that he didn't seem more distraught.

"So you see," he continued, "you and I have much to commiserate about if we choose to do so." He smiled. "But I hope we won't."

He reached up and smoothed the backs of his fingers down the curve of her jaw. "My first reaction," he said, "was wanting to curl up in a ball and just... fade away. But my grandfather, wise man that he is, helped me to put it all into perspective." He paused to take a deep breath.

"I am not—" he stopped suddenly and corrected "—you and I are not defined by the circumstances of our births. And I firmly believe, Lyssa, that Kit-tan-it-to'wet, The Great Holy One, brought us together because no one could teach us that lesson better than each other. Don't you think?"

It was a rhetorical question.

His tone was feather soft as he declared, "We were meant to be. To face the past, the present, and the future. Together."

Her heart soared with hope. She was so tired.

Running from the secret of her past had been exhausting. Fleeing the disaster she'd made of her life had left her feeling drained. But sitting here in the moonlight with the love of her life, she suddenly had the stamina of a marathon athlete, ready to sprint toward her future. A future with Dakota.

"I love you, Lyssa. You're not just the woman of my heart. You're the woman of my soul. I've been stubborn about the lesson, but I've finally learned that I would be incomplete without you."

The tremulous emotions raging within her were overwhelming. Overpowering. Desire smoldered like glowing embers in the deepest part of her being.

Dakota slid his hand over her belly in a most intimate fashion. "I want us to raise your baby—our baby— just as I was raised by my father, Will Makwa. I want to love this child as I was loved. Wholly. Unreservedly."

His unconditional acceptance of her and her baby had an awesome impact on her. Tears welled and spilled with each blink.

"Oh, Dakota," she whispered. "I love you so much."

The trust she'd held prisoner for so very long finally broke free. Dakota knew all her secrets, and still he loved her. Her heart, her very soul, opened to him like the petals of a delicate flower.

She fell into his arms, ready to race toward all their tomorrows.

EPILOGUE

February roared over the mountainous Vermont landscape like a lion. Two days of icy snow and wind had everyone feeling blue about being trapped indoors for days at a time... everyone, that was, but Lyssa.

She'd relished the lazy afternoons spent reclining by the fire with her husband. She'd never been happier in her life. Yes, the end of her pregnancy was approaching and the baby was growing to the extent that she was beginning to feel uncomfortable. Still, she met every day with a contented smile.

The rich scent of beef and vegetables filled the kitchen. A loaf of freshly baked bread sat cooling on the counter. Lyssa stirred the stew and then went to set the table. Dakota should be home any minute.

A series of storms had dumped nearly a foot of snow on Misty Glen Reservation and the surrounding area. Cell phone reception all over the rez had been spotty most of the day, and Dakota had gone over to check on his grandfather. He and Mat were planning on shoveling the snow so that Grayson could more easily get to and from his home.

Lyssa had taken advantage of this time alone to prepare Dakota a nice, stick-to-your-bones meal. They would eat together, share a little conversation, then... they'd enjoy dessert in bed.

She grinned, her face flaming as desire coursed throughout her swollen body. Most women spent the final stages of pregnancy feeling fat and ugly, but thanks to Dakota's effusive affection, Lyssa felt beautiful, glowing, and happy. She couldn't help but think she was the luckiest woman in the whole world.

The first pain seemed to come out of nowhere, knifing across her stomach and her lower back at the same time. The magnitude of it was such that she dropped the bowls she'd been carrying to the table. The ceramic dishes smashed to the floor, shattering into several chunky pieces.

Gulping in a lungful of air, she realized that the contraction had hit her so hard that she hadn't even thought to utter the groan that had gathered in the back of her throat.

She clutched the chair back until the wave passed. Then she waited, frightened and shaking. Never had it entered her mind that bringing her child into the world would bring so much pain that it couldn't be tolerated. Women gave birth every day and survived the experience just fine. But the enormity of that surprising contraction had packed such a wallop that doubt filled her thoughts with clouds. Ominous ones.

The pain faded. Seconds ticked by, turning into minutes. And when the first spasm wasn't followed by a second, Lyssa heaved a sigh of relief.

"False labor," she whispered to herself, gently rubbing her round belly for good measure.

She looked down at the clutter of broken stoneware and grimaced. Just as she bent to pick up the pieces, she was hit with another monstrous contraction. This one brought her to her knees.

The moan she emitted sounded so traumatic to her own ears that her fear escalated. Suddenly dizzy, she sank onto her bottom, panting as she was hit with concentric surges of gripping pangs. Moisture slowly spread into a puddle around her on the tile floor and her eyes widened. Her water had broken. There was nothing false about this labor. The baby was coming.

Soon.

The next forty odd minutes that passed seemed like hours. All Lyssa knew was that she had to hang on. She tried desperately not to pass out from the agony of what nature was doing to her body... and she prayed for Dakota to arrive.

And he did.

Almost as if he knew she was in need of him, he pushed his way through the front door, tapped the snow off his boots, and called her name. She frantically shouted for him and he was at her side in an instant.

"Something's wrong," she told him, knowing that her breathing was erratic and that perspiration glistened on her forehead and upper lip. "It's coming fast. Too fast."

"Sometimes babies do," he crooned, smoothing

a comforting hand over her hair. He did a quick check and grinned up at her. "The baby's head is crowning. I see lots of silky dark hair."

"I can't give birth on the kitchen floor!"

He was so calm, drat him. She was a nurse. She should be calm, too. She'd read all the books, attended birthing classes. She was prepared.

But not for this, she decided as she was wracked with yet another colossal contraction.

"Dakota," she panted, "this can't be happening... first deliveries are supposed to take hours."

Her husband chuckled. "Some women would call you lucky." Then he ordered, "Focus on your breathing. Look at me."

She did as he bid, gazing into his wonderful eyes. One more mind-blowing pain brought her son into the world, and it wasn't too much longer before she was nestled in the comfort of her bed, cradling her baby boy in her arms.

"He's beautiful," Dakota whispered. "He looks just like you."

Lyssa could only smile. She was overjoyed to be holding this child she'd waited for and anticipated for months.

"What are we going to call him?" Dakota

smoothed his fingertips down the baby's nose and chin, and he was rewarded when his son's little bow-shaped mouth pursed.

Before Lyssa could answer, Dakota suggested, "How about Lucky?" He chuckled. "That's it! Lucky Snowstorm Makwa."

Even though she knew he was teasing, she clicked her tongue in chastisement. "Lucky is what you name your favorite beagle, not your baby boy." Then she looked up into his moss-green eyes, shyly adding, "I was thinking of naming him Grayson. Do you think your grandfather would mind?' '

"Mind? I think Grandfather will be in heaven!" He leaned over and kissed her lips, and Lyssa felt warmed through with the feeling of being loved. She watched Dakota plant a gentle kiss on their son's fuzzy dark head and she knew the true meaning of honest-to-goodness contentment.

THE END

Although the books in this series are stand-alone novels, reading the books in order will offer the most enjoyable experience. Titles in The Black Bear Brothers Series:

An Honorable Man, Book 1
Woman of His Heart, Book 2
Healing Chay, Book 3

Page forward for a note from the author.

A Note From The Author

Dear Reader,

When I first began writing Woman of His Heart, Dakota's problem felt a little farfetched to me—a man too handsome to remain single? Ha! But then it seemed that every day there was another story on the news about sexual harassment, and it quickly became clear to me how one hint of gossip could easily ruin a doctor's reputation. Suddenly, Dakota's situation didn't seem so outlandish, after all. And I felt his willingness to help Lyssa out with *her* problem only made him more appealing.

I hope you enjoyed Woman of His Heart. If you did, please consider leaving a short review. And please tell a friend! Nothing helps an author more than word-of-mouth recommendations.

The Black Bear Brothers series has 2 more books:

Mat's story: An Honorable Man, Book 1

Chay's story: Healing Chay, Book 3

Both books are available as e-books and as paperbacks. I'd be honored if you would look for them.

All my best,

Donna Fasano

Other Books By Donna Fasano

The Ocean City Boardwalk Series:
(Contemporary Romance)
Following His Heart, Book 1
Two Hearts in Winter, Book 2
Wild Hearts of Summer, Book 3
An Almost Perfect Christmas, Book 4
Grown-Up Christmas List, Book 5
The Wedding Planner's Son, Book 6
Second Chance Valentine, Book 7
Her Mr. Miracle, Book 8

The Single Daddy Club:
(Sweet Romance)
Derrick, Book 1
Jason, Book 2
Reece, Book 3

Stand-Alone Novels:
Finding Fiona (Women's Fiction)
The Merry-Go-Round (Romantic Comedy)
Reclaim My Heart (Contemporary Romance)
Mountain Laurel (Sweet Romance)
Take Me, I'm Yours (Contemporary Romance)
Her Fake Romance (Contemporary Romance)

A Family Forever Series:
(Sweet Romance, can be read as stand-alone
novels)
A Beautiful Stranger, Book 1
Made in Paradise, Book 2
A Reason to Believe, Book 3
An Accidental Family, Book 4
Nanny and the Professor, Book 5

Non-Fiction:
The Prayer of Quiet
Cooking in all Directions: Recipes from the Blog
Favorite Christmas Cookies
Guy Food

About The Author

Donna Fasano is a USA TODAY Bestselling Author whose books have sold 4 million copies worldwide and have been translated into two dozen languages. She and her husband live on Maryland's Eastern Shore.